Next Teller

A Book of Canadian Storytelling

Collected by Dan Yashinsky

RAGWEED
THE ISLAND PUBLISHER

Artwork on cover and section pages: Soozi Schlanger
Printed and bound in Canada by: Webcom

Acknowledgements: Thanks to the following publishers for kind permission to reprint the following stories in this collection: "Jack Fury," from Joe Neil MacNeil's *Tales Until Dawn*, translated and edited by John Shaw (McGill-Queen's University Press: 1987); *Name Calling*, Itah Sadu (Well Versed Publications: 1992); "The Sound of Dancing," from Alexander Wolfe's *Earth Elder Stories* (Fifth House: 1988).

Ragweed Press acknowledges the generous support of the Canada Council and the Department of Canadian Heritage, Multiculturalism.

Published by
Ragweed Press
P.O. Box 2023
Charlottetown, P.E.I.
Canada   C1A 7N7

Distributors
Canada: General Distribution Services
United States: Inland Book Company
United Kingdom: Turnaround Distribution

Canadian Cataloguing in Publication Data

Main entry under title:

Next teller

   ISBN 0-921556-46-2

1. Short stories, Canadian (English) * 2. Canadian fiction (English) — 20th century. * I. Yashinsky, Dan, 1950 -

PS8321.N69 1994   C813'.0108054   C94-950052-6
PR9197.32.N69 1994

▼▼▼▼▼▼

To Alice Kane,
who likes to remind storytellers that
"'tis a poor heart that never rejoices."

▼▼▼

Contents

▶ **Prologue**   1

▶ **Curious Children**   5
Voiceover   7
The Curious Girl   *Kay Stone*   8
Old Frost and Young Frost   *Celia Barker Lottridge*   15
Down by the Water's Edge   *Bernadette Dyer*   20
Boy   *Steve Altstedter*   25
The Orphan Who Became a Great Shaman
    Pat Andrews   33
Name Calling   *Itah Sadu*   37
Ti-Jean and His Three Little Pigs   *Camille Perron*   42
The Mysterious Singing Drum   *Bob Barton*   52

▶ **Tricksters**   63
Voiceover   65
Reynard and Chanticleer   *Melanie Ray*   66
Jack Fury   *Joe Neil MacNeil*
    (translated by *John Shaw*)   71
The Devil's Noodles   *Dan Yashinsky*   81
The Raccoon Story   *Lynda Howes*   91
Nanabush Stories   *Gilbert Oskaboose*   97
How Trickster Brought Fire to the People
    Lenore Keeshig-Tobias   106

‣ **Lovers**   **115**

Voiceover   117

Va Attacher la Vache!   *Justin Lewis*   118

The Wall of Glass   *Deanne Mallard*   124

The Third Wish   *Ricky Zurif*   128

The Legend of Lady Meng   *Frieda Ling*   135

The Legend of Lupi the Great White Wolf
    Esther Jacko   143

‣ **Hauntings**   **165**

Voiceover   167

The Loup-Garou and the Shawl   *Marylyn Peringer*   168

Ozzie Hardin and the Feu Follet   *Steve Luxton*   175

The Lady in the Snow   *J. Antonin Friolet*   180

Maggie Lochlin's Last Storm   *Teresa Doyle*   187

The Ghost Ship   *Jocelyn Bérubé*
    (translated by Shawna Watson)   192

No-Post   *Nan Gregory*   197

Bag o' Bones   *Louis Bird*   201

The Little Boy in the Tree   *Basil Johnston, O.Ont.*   206

The Sound of Dancing   *Alexander Wolfe*   216

‣ **Tellers' Tales**   **223**

Voiceover   225

How to Tell a Story   *Robert Minden*   226

Grimaldi   *Carmen Orlandis-Habsburgo*   228

Almost Dying   *Ken Roberts*   232

Andrew's Wolf Pups   *René Fumoleau*   235

‣ **Biographical Notes**   **241**

Prologue

There's this sign at my bank. I've always wanted to take it. The sign says "Next Teller," and the workers at the bank put it up when they're so busy counting other people's money that they haven't time to bother with mine.

I like that sign because it reminds me of why people tell stories. To be a storyteller means knowing stories in your head. It means knowing how to say them out loud, getting the words right, making pictures with your words. And it especially means finding the "next" teller. Your story has to find a new home in the listener's memory and voice. It has to spark across the gap into another person's life. All storytellers are searching for you, the one who will keep their stories alive, the one who is next in a long line of rememberers and re-tellers.

I never have been able to get the sign from the bank. They might have just given it to me, but I've always been too shy to ask (it's amazing how shy storytellers can be, since we're not afraid to get up in front of people and talk). So, instead, I went ahead and borrowed it for the title of this book.

This is a collection of stories from storytellers living in Canada. The stories are all being told today by the people who gave me permission to put them in this book. They tell the stories in small villages, on northern traplines, in downtown coffee houses, in seacoast outports and onstage at storytelling festivals. The tales come from many traditions and cultures:

1

Cree, Dene, Ojibway, Chinese, English, Québécois, Franco-Ontarian, Acadian, Gaelic, Jewish, Jamaican and others. Even so, they are only a very small part of the mighty patchwork quilt of stories Canadians create every day. My joy in putting this book together has been in hearing so many fine stories; my regret is that I couldn't include more of them. But this first volume of *Next Teller* is only the first step in what I hope will be a lifelong story-gathering journey across Canada.

Who are the storytellers in this book? They include Native elders, local raconteurs, stand-up comics, librarians, professional storytellers and writers, a priest, a trapper, a high-school English student, a clown, a Judo teacher, a folklorist and many others. There is, for example, Joe Neil MacNeil from Big Pond, Cape Breton. I once heard him recite a Gaelic proverb: "What the ear does not hear will not move the heart." He has spent his life holding stories clear in his memory so that new listeners can hear and be moved by them. There is Esther Jacko from Birch Island Indian Reserve, who made sure to get her grandmother's permission before writing down the legend of "Lupi the Great White Wolf." There is Louis Bird, who travels around James Bay on his snowmobile taping the Cree elders. At last count, he has more than thirty cassettes of ancient Cree history, legends and philosophy. All of these storytellers are my heroes.

Storytelling is hero's work. Nowadays we have many books, microchips, videos, databases — more information than anyone could ever use. But we know very few stories by heart, stories to pass along by word of mouth. The storyteller teaches us that we're responsible for keeping our stories alive. It's not enough to leave them in a computer or on a videotape or even in a book. The brave part of storytelling, the part that takes imagination and high spirits and a bit of luck, is when

2

you say that you're the one who'll remember. You take responsibility for making sure the stories don't disappear.

One of the storytellers in this book, Gilbert Oskaboose from Serpent River First Nation, wrote me a bittersweet letter about how modern storytellers must work to hold on to their stories. Here, with his permission, is his letter:

> It would be nice to tell you a pretty story of the ancient legends of the Ojibway and how they are told and retold, passed down from generation to generation ... It would be nice to weave a wild-eyed and wondrous tale of long winter nights and crackling fires and children spellbound ... I'd dearly love to tell of great steaming mugs of hot tea, the aroma of pipe tobacco and the gentle murmur of Ojibway voices in the night ...
>
> My soul cries out to tell you these things but my voice remains silent — because these things are no more. There is a proverb amongst my people: When the legends die the people are lost. The Ojibway are lost ...
>
> And yet, a strange thing ... every time I make that awful pronouncement I hear — somewhere deep in the shadows of my mind — something that sounds suspiciously like a snicker. I think it's that rascal Nanabush — and he's trying to tell me something.
>
> I think he's trying to tell me that things will be okay. The legends may be dying in my community, but there are other villages, other storytellers ...
>
> I think he's trying to tell me that change is okay, that if our language and oral traditions of storytelling are dying away, then it's all right to store the tales on a floppy disk for a while.
>
> There will be another Storyteller ... and another ...
> — The Moon of the Changing Leaves, 1990

Gilbert Oskaboose is my hero.

There's an order to *Next Teller:* The book begins with stories about children who must discover great powers to overcome grave dangers. Then come tales about tricksters, some — like Jack Fury — all too human; and some endowed with world-making, world-transforming power, like Nanabush. Men and women are next, with stories about how we love and *mis*love each other. Some of these tales are sad, some funny, some — like the incredible epic of "Lupi the Great White Wolf" — touched by demonic horror. These stories are followed by a section of fine, spooky ghost tales. The last stories in the book are about death, dying and gaining wisdom. The book ends with "Andrew's Wolf Pups," a true-life experience Andrew the Dene trapper told to René Fumoleau about raising some wolf cubs and losing them back to the wilderness one day. Growing up, learning to use your wits, meeting Worldmaker in his/her Trickster shape, loving and misloving, facing death — and letting your wolves go free. That's how the book moves. But if you're like me, you probably don't read collections of stories straight through — you meander; you jump around; you read whatever catches your eye. That's a good way to read *Next Teller.*

The storytellers have written introductions to their tales, which you'll find at the beginning of each story. In them, you can learn about where the stories are from and how the tellers learned them. You can find out more about the storytellers in the notes at the back of the book.

If you like a story you read here, it will start to belong to you. If you remember it after you put the book down, then you've given it a home. And if you re-tell it to a new listener, then you've become the Next Teller.

Dan Yashinsky

Curious
Children

▼▼▼▼▼▼

Voiceover

The children in these stories get themselves in and out of serious trouble. They look in secret windows, steal candy from stern adults, stray down deserted beaches, and give away precious livestock for a peek at a girl's leg. If everybody followed all the rules all the time, there would be less trouble in this world but there would also be fewer stories. To make a story, someone must do something out of the ordinary. The children here all take extraordinary risks. Sometimes these are foolish risks, and sometimes they are necessary; from both kinds the children gain knowledge about themselves and the world they live in.

You must take risks to learn how to grow up. You must earn your powers. The stories that follow are about children who discover both how low they can tumble, and how high they can soar.

The Curious Girl

Kay Stone

"A Dutch-born friend of mine uses an expression for storytelling that she learned in her own family: 'shaking it out of your sleeve.' I've been fascinated by her words because I have learned, from years of telling, that a good story arises with the spontaneity of something that seems to appear naturally, so familiar that it is always at hand and yet at the same time seems to appear magically, like a rabbit in a hat or an ace up a sleeve. Like magicians and cardsharps, storytellers have to be very well-prepared before they can be spontaneous. By itself, an empty sleeve yields neither stories nor aces. We storytellers prepare ourselves with years of conscious and unconscious listening, learning and exchanging stories before we can share our art with confidence.

I love to tell stories, but writing them down is much more difficult for me. The story I offer here should have been easy to put down in print since I've been telling it for a few years and know it well. But when I sat down to solidify my words into print, they refused to flow. Frozen things do not flow. I had to find some way of allowing them to thaw again and find a new form. If this makes no sense to you, try writing down a joke you love to tell, or some amusing or annoying experience you've shared with friends or family. Try freezing it into print and you will understand my difficulties. Shaking it out of your sleeve becomes more challenging because spontaneity is more difficult to achieve when your listeners are not present. Writers have to imagine an audience — and so I imagine you, reading these words that I shake out of my sleeve.

The story of *The Curious Girl* is a little known Grimm tale that appears in English translations as 'Frau Trude' or 'Dame Trudy.' When I first read it, I was so angry that I threw my book across the room, enraged that a girl who was merely curious (as I was) and disobedient was turned into a log and burned by a witch. But the story fascinated me, and refused to let me go free. I began telling the story to discover if there was something up its sleeve, and there was. Not a rabbit, but a bird — as you will see."

▼▼▼

Once there was a girl who was stubborn and curious and disobedient to her parents. Whenever they told her to do one thing she'd do another.

Now how could a girl like that *not* get into trouble? And she did.

One day she said to her parents, "I think I'll visit Mother Trudy. They say she lives in an interesting house full of strange things, and I'm curious to see her."

Her parents protested. They said, "Mother Trudy is a godless woman who does evil things, and if you go there you will be our child no longer!"

But the Curious Girl did not listen.

Without another word to her parents, she set off through the woods. Soon she crossed a small stream, and when she stepped onto the other shore, the woods around her seemed dark and dismal.

As she walked along, the Curious Girl felt a trembling beneath her feet, and a sound like rolling thunder coming from behind her. She turned to look — and saw a dark rider on a dark horse roaring toward her. She leapt aside just as horse and rider galloped by.

When they had passed, darkness fell all around and she could no longer see her way. But she continued on, feeling the path beneath her feet.

After some time, the earth began to tremble and shake. The Curious Girl heard a raging sound behind her and turned to see an enormous rider on a horse that burned red like the rising sun. Once again, horse and rider came speeding toward her, and again she leapt aside as they raced on by. After they had passed, the sky above the dark trees became blood red.

Now the Curious Girl was frightened, but she continued on her way. After some time, she again heard a deafening sound behind her and turned, this time to see a brilliant white rider on a white horse flashing toward her. She threw herself out of their path. When they had passed by, bright day glowed all around and the Curious Girl found herself in a clearing.

And there, in the very heart of the dark forest, was a strange house, just as she had heard. It was small and plain, but it had an odd feeling about it that made her uneasy. Then she saw that the house was surrounded by a fence made of human bones; and in front of the house was a small tree with leaves the colour of blood. The Curious Girl was terrified, but she was also determined. She crept up to the house and looked in the window. There, she was astounded to see the figure of a woman, all in flames but not consumed.

Then the Curious Girl heard her name called. A voice commanded her to enter the house. In a trance, she stepped around to the door, pushed it slowly inward, and stepped inside.

What she saw there was an ordinary old woman sitting in an extraordinary chair. The chair had the legs of a strange animal. The old woman was Mother Trudy, and she looked at the Curious Girl with piercing eyes. Finally, the old woman spoke politely: "My dear, why are you so pale and shaking?"

"Because I've seen such strange things!" the Curious Girl answered, breathlessly.

"Oh? What have you seen?"

"As I was walking I saw a huge dark rider on a dark horse."

"That was only my Dark Night," said Mother Trudy.

"Then I saw an enormous red rider on a red horse."

"Yes, that was my Red Morning."

"Then there was a white rider on a white horse, flashing like lightning."

"Indeed, that was my Bright Day. And what else did you see, my dear?"

"Oh, then I looked in your window, Mother Trudy, but I didn't see you at all — I saw a woman all in flames."

"Did you now! Then you have seen the witch in her true form. I have been waiting for you and longing for you. You will burn brightly for me." And so saying, Mother Trudy turned the girl into a log and threw the log on her fire. As the fire blazed, she sat down next to it and said to herself, "Indeed, it does burn brightly."

Suddenly a shower of sparks flew out of the fire and into the air. Mother Trudy sprang up and changed the sparks into a fiery bird with feathers like the rising sun, a beak as black as night and eyes that flashed like summer lightning. Then she caught that bird and held it firmly.

"Clever girl!" she said. "But you'll never get away from me! You will remain a bird forever and my servant for all eternity — unless you can fulfill my bargain: If you can tell me one story that I've never heard before, a story that has no ending, I'll let you go. If you cannot, you will be in my power forever."

"That's not fair," replied the Curious Girl. "You know many more stories than I do."

"That is true," said the old woman. "So I'll give you all the time you need to learn more. Go anywhere you like. Return to me when you're ready. I will be waiting for you. If you fail you'll be mine forever." She carried the bird outside, lifted her hand high, and released it into the air. The bird flew up — and a red flash disappeared into the dark woods.

As she flew, the Curious Girl thought of all the languages she could speak in her new shape, knowing that the birds understand the speech of all living things, even the stones on the path (for some stones are alive). And so she began her long wandering in the world, flying everywhere, learning stories from all she met.

She went to the east where the sun rises and to the west where it sets; she went to the white north and to the green south; she went to the mountains and the seas, the forests and the barren lands. She heard the trees and all other growing things, even the tiniest flowers; she listened to the birds and all the other creatures who could fly, and to all the creatures who could creep, walk, leap, or swim. She wandered through farms and villages, towns and cities, learning stories from everyone who lived there, young and old alike. And she did not forget to listen to the stones on the path.

Much time passed as the Curious Girl wandered in the form of the fiery bird. And while her outer shape did not change, inside she grew older with the years, until finally she had matured into a woman. At times she was so enraptured by the stories she heard that she almost forgot Mother Trudy — but her enchanted state as a bird always reminded her of her task. And so at last she returned to the strange house in the forest. As she hovered overhead, she saw the circle made by the fence of bones, and she saw also the blood red tree growing near the house. It had been only a sapling when she'd first seen it.

On the day that the Curious Girl returned, Mother Trudy heard a strange song outside her house. She went to see who was singing and found the fiery bird in the tree. "Ah, it's you," she said. "I've been waiting. Have you brought me a story?"

"I have all the stories in the world to tell you!"

"Good," Mother Trudy answered. "I haven't heard a fine tale for a long time. Begin."

The Curious Girl, who was now a woman, told Mother Trudy the stories she'd learned from all of creation. Some were short and some long, some were plain and others fancy, some comic and others tragic, but they all carried truth in them.

When she had finished, Mother Trudy gazed at the fiery bird intently and exclaimed, "Ah yes, excellent stories, and well told too … But I knew every one of them long before you were born!"

The Curious Girl was speechless. She had no more stories. None at all. But when she opened her mouth to cry out, words came out on their own, one at a time at first and then running together like a small river: "Once there was a girl who was stubborn and curious, and disobedient to her parents. Whenever they told her to do one thing she'd do another …"

And that was the story that had never been heard, the story without an end.

Old Frost and Young Frost
Celia Barker Lottridge

"This is a Lithuanian story, but all who live in cold
countries will recognize Young Frost and his father.
Take a walk in the snowy forest or down a windy city
street and you will meet them. Do you know what to
do? The poor woodcutter may teach you a few tricks."

You already know Old Frost. He's the one who sends shivers
down your spine on cold winter days. He nips your toes and
makes the tip of your nose turn red. Yes, you know Old Frost,
but you may not know that he has a son called Young Frost.
Like all sons, Young Frost likes to believe he is much more
clever than his father. In fact, there are times when Young
Frost thinks that he should be doing Old Frost's job himself.

On one such day Old Frost and Young Frost were sitting
up in a tree in the snowy forest. As usual, Young Frost was
begging for a chance to show how quickly he could make
people sorry that they had ventured away from their cozy
fires. He paused as a shiny sleigh pulled by a pair of well-fed
horses passed beneath the tree. Inside the sleigh was a rich
merchant, as well-fed as his horses and wrapped in furs. He
wore fur-lined boots, a thick fur coat, a fur hat pulled well

15

down over his ears, and he was covered by a shaggy fur blanket.

"Look at that one," said Young Frost. "He thinks he is safe from chills and shivers. Just give me a chance. I'll show you what I can do."

"All right," said his father, "go ahead. Show me."

Young Frost zipped down the tree and into the sleigh. He wound himself around the merchant's neck, looking for a little opening where he could slip in. And he found one, just at the back of the thick fur collar of the coat. Down he went, right down the man's back.

The man began to shiver. "Drive faster! Do you want me to freeze?" he shouted at the driver. He huddled into his coat, trying to wrap himself more tightly in the fur. But Young Frost had found his way into the wide tops of the boots and was busy nipping the man's toes. After that, he squeezed under the flaps of the fur hat and turned the merchant's ears bright red. Then he hung around, giving a shiver here and a nip there.

When the merchant reached home he was so cold he could hardly move. His wife had to sit him by the fire and feed him hot soup and tea.

Young Frost flew back to the tree, laughing. "Did you see what I did?" he said to Old Frost. "All those furs meant nothing to me. That man won't forget me soon."

Old Frost smiled his thin smile and the air crackled with cold.

"You did not do badly," he said, "not badly at all. Of course, that was an easy job." Young Frost was outraged but his father went on, "Sensible people know it takes more than fur to keep them warm when Frost is in the forest. Now if you really want to show what you can do, try him." And he pointed a long finger at a woodcutter who was guiding his sledge beneath the tree.

Young Frost looked down. He saw a man dressed in a thin padded coat, ancient felt boots, worn leather mitts and a hat that had been furry long ago. His sledge was made of logs roughly nailed together and his horse was old and bony. He had an axe lying beside him. Anyone could see that he was going into the forest to cut wood.

"That one!" said Young Frost. "It will take no time to send him shivering home." But Old Frost just shook his head. "You can try," he said.

Young Frost slid down from the tree into the sledge. He quickly found a worn place in one of the woodcutter's felt boots and squeezed through it. He planned to give the woodcutter's toes a good nip but he had hardly begun before the man hopped out of the sledge and began running along beside his horse.

Young Frost was sure that he was going to be trampled inside the boot, but, just in time, he managed to find his way out of the hole. When he was safe he flew along behind the woodcutter, waiting for him to climb back into the sledge.

When he did, Young Frost was ready. He had spied a spot in the padded coat where a button was missing. He slid through the gap and settled down to send chills up the man's chest, around his neck and down his back. But with the very first shiver of cold the man dropped the reins and began pounding his chest with his fists.

Young Frost had to hop to avoid getting thumped. No matter what cozy place he found, the pounding fists found him. It wasn't long before Young Frost was out in the fresh air, shaking his head.

"Never mind," he said to himself. "Just wait until he starts cutting wood. Then I'll get him." He had his eye on the woodcutter's ears where they stuck out below the flaps of his old fur hat.

The woodcutter stopped the horse in a little clearing among the trees and jumped out of the sledge with his axe in his hand, ready to get to work. Young Frost was ready too, but the woodcutter started chopping so furiously that wood chips flew everywhere. Young Frost couldn't get near those ears.

He was flying around thinking of how Old Frost would laugh, when the woodcutter paused to push his hat back from his forehead. "This work warms a man up," he remarked and, as if to prove it, he took off his mitts and threw them on the seat of the sledge. Then he gripped the axe and went back to his chopping.

Young Frost could not believe his luck. "I'll creep inside those mitts and make them so cold that he'll start to shiver as soon as he sticks his fingers in them. Then he'll forget all his wretched tricks and I'll have him." And Young Frost got busy inside the mitts.

The woodcutter went on chopping until he had filled the sledge with neatly cut logs. Then he put down his axe and picked up his mitts. They were frozen stiff. The man shook his head and slapped the mitts together. They rang like iron. He looked at the mitts and at his hands and shook his head again. "It's a terrible frost today," he said. "But I can cure it." He laid the mitts on the stump of a tree, picked up his axe and began to pound the mitts with the flat side of the axe.

He pounded until his mitts were soft again. Young Frost barely escaped with his life. He was so bruised and sore that he found a chink in the pile of logs and stayed there until the sledge passed under the tree where Old Frost waited. Even then he could barely fly up to the branch.

"What a terrible man!" he said to his father. "First he trampled me, then he thumped me, then he hit me with pieces of wood and finally he pounded me with an axe. You can have that job. I don't want it."

Old Frost laughed until the air glittered. "When you can outsmart a poor woodcutter who gets his living outdoors in all weathers, you'll be ready to take over my job," he said. "But, until then, it is the woodcutter and I who rule the winter forest."

Down by the Water's Edge
Bernadette Dyer

"Every time I think about the story *Down By The Water's Edge*, it takes me back to my early childhood when I was growing up in a remote part of the island of Jamaica in the West Indies. It was a place called Serge Island. Serge Island wasn't really an island at all, but was surrounded by two rivers. One was called the Johnson River and the other, the Negro River. In Serge Island there was a sugar estate and sweeping landscapes including streams, meadows, pastures, hills and gullies.

Besides farmhouses, there were modest-sized homes, small cottages and shacks. But there was also a large mansion, perhaps left over from the slavery days, which was known locally as 'The Great House!' For me, Serge Island was a magical place, the place where all the stories started. Our family was fortunate enough to have hired household help which included cooks, washers, cleaners and gardeners. These wonderful helpers were prolific storytellers, filling us children with the drama of 'Duppy Stories,' 'Anancy Stories,' and all manner of local Jamaican folklore and legends.

Now that I think back on it, storytelling for them was so natural that to read stories would have been unheard of. The oral tradition was broad and rich amongst field workers, sugar cane labourers and even donkey-cart men.

Even today, I can well remember the phrase: 'Did you hear the story about …' Serge also brings back delicious sounding names such as Hallhead, Sodom, Danvers Pen, Cedar Valley and Coley. As you might see, *Down By The Water's Edge* is full of images that for me will always be a part of Serge Island in Jamaica."

▼▼▼

A long time ago in the islands of the Caribbean, there lived two little sisters. One sister was very beautiful, but the other was as plain as plain can be. The beautiful sister was not very helpful or kind, and never did as she was told. It was always the plain sister who was kind, and helped with the housework from dawn to dusk.

Now back in those days there was no running water in the houses, so it was children who were sent to fetch water from the rivers or wells. The plain sister did this quite often. She would take her bucket and cross the lush countryside. But the river was a fair distance from where she lived, and in order to get there she had to walk through many fields and meadows and small forests. Once she reached the river, there was a steep cliff with sharp jutting rocks along the edges and lush ferns growing out from the crevices. The plain sister would carefully climb down those treacherous rocks with her bucket, slip cautiously through the ferns and make her way to the shore below.

One day, as the plain sister was lowering herself carefully, she was surprised to see that there, sitting amongst the rocks and ferns, was the ugliest old woman it was possible to imagine! The old woman was covered with lumps and bumps, and on her back was a huge hump, and her face was covered with warts. The plain sister was frightened, but she did not show her fear. She continued to climb down, clutching the bucket. All of a sudden the old woman turned and saw her.

"Little girl," she said, "could you please scratch my back?"

Now the plain sister was very frightened but, since she always did as she was told, she went to the old woman, and she scratched her back. She scratched the old woman's back, and she scratched the old woman's back, and she scratched the old woman's back; but still the old woman asked for it to be scratched some more. Her back was hard and brittle as broken glass. Soon, as the girl scratched, her fingers ached and ran with blood. But still the old woman asked for more. So she scratched the old woman's back until finally the old woman said, "Little girl, could you get me a drink of water?"

The plain sister was still frightened, but she didn't show her fear and, since she always did as she was told, she made her way down to the water's edge. She dipped her bucket into the water. Then, finding an old empty calabash nearby, she poured the water into the calabash. Finally she climbed up the steep incline to where the old woman was, and gave her the water. The old woman drank thirstily. Then she spoke: "Little girl, you have been kind to an old woman. What can I give you in return?"

The plain sister felt suddenly shy, and replied, "Your blessing is all I ask."

The old woman smiled. "Little girl," she said, "go down to the river and get your water and you will see what you will see."

The plain sister climbed carefully through the rocks and ferns to the water's edge. She lowered her bucket into the water, but when she tried to pull it out, the bucket felt heavier than usual. She tugged at it and tugged at it with all her might, and finally she pulled it out. To her amazement, she could see that the bucket was heaping with diamonds and precious stones. So she peered into the water and saw, looking back at her, a most beautiful little girl. When she moved her head, the girl in the water moved her head also. She moved her arm, and the girl in the water moved her arm. It took the plain sister only a moment to realize that she and the girl in the water were one and the same, and suddenly it occurred to her what must have happened. But when she turned to thank the old woman, she found her gone.

Once again the girl climbed up the steep rock face, this time carrying her bucket of jewels. She walked through the forests and fields and meadows until she came to her village. As she drew near to her home, her unkind sister saw her coming. The unkind sister could hardly believe that the lovely young girl with the bucket could be her plain sister. And she was even more amazed when she saw the jewels. "What happened to you?" she gasped.

"Something happened down by the river," the girl replied.

Before she could finish her story, however, the unkind sister grabbed a bucket of her own and raced off through the fields and meadows and forests towards the river. When she came to the place with the steep cliff, she slid through the ferns, barely managing to escape the sharp rocks. And then, just ahead of her, she saw sitting amongst the rocks the ugliest old woman it was possible to imagine. The old woman was covered with lumps and bumps, and on her back was a huge hump, and her face was covered with warts.

Although she was somewhat surprised to see an old woman there, the unkind sister hurried on her way, more determined than ever to get to the water's edge. She was taken aback when the old woman called out to her, "Little girl, could you please scratch my back?"

Ignoring the old woman, the unkind sister pressed on, calling back sharply, "Scratch your own back. Can't you see that I am in a hurry." With that, she continued her descent.

The old woman called out again, "Little girl, could you get me a drink of water?"

The unkind sister was angry now, and paused before replying to the old woman. "Didn't you hear me the first time?" she sneered. "I have no time to do things for you. I have much more important things to do." And so saying, she scampered through the rocks until she stood by the water's edge. Immediately, she lowered her bucket into the swirling waters.

The bucket felt heavier than she expected, so she tugged and tugged at it with all her might. At last the bucket came up. It was heaped with frogs, toads, snails and worms, and all the slimy, creeping things from the river bed. Then, there in the water, she saw a great big claw moving. She moved her arm, and the claw moved. She moved her foot, and another great big claw in the water moved. She moved her head, and saw tiny black eyes on a huge head looking back at her. It took her only a moment to realize that she was seeing a giant crab, and that she and the crab were one and the same.

And from that day until this, the unkind sister is living as a crab down in the mud at the water's edge, and no one will scratch her back.

Boy

Steve Altstedter

"I first heard this story as a child at Judo class. It somehow stayed with me and as the years passed and I taught Judo classes of my own, I retold this story again and again. I hope you enjoy it."

▼▼▼

Many years ago in far-off Japan, there was a boy named Koji. Most children in Japan are polite, well-mannered and respectful — but not Koji. No, Koji was always getting into trouble, and his parents did not know what to do. Whenever he caused trouble they had to pay for the damages, and they were very poor. They could not afford all these payments. Of course, Koji would apologize and promise to be good, but he always got himself into trouble once again.

Finally, Koji's father decided that Koji must go and stay with the monks in the monastery nearby, who sometimes took in boys to help with their work. So the father took his son by the hand and left him at the gate of the monastery.

Soon the heavy gate moved. "What is your name, boy," asked the monk who opened the gate.

"Koji-chan, Master," answered Koji.

"Well, Koji-chan, I am the master of this monastery, and

all who live here obey when I speak. Come with me and you can work here."

So Koji followed the Headmaster into the monastery. He was shown a place on the floor in a room where he would sleep. Other boys were there too, and they all shared the same room. Koji was told that there would be two meals a day: soup and a bowl of rice for breakfast, and fish and rice for supper. His work was to clean up around the buildings and sometimes help out in the fields.

Days passed and the work was hard. The monks in the monastery treated the boys cruelly. They were beaten unjustly, and if any of them complained to the Headmaster, they were punished all the more for creating disharmony. Koji woke up at dawn each morning and fell into an exhausted sleep at sunset. But in spite of all this, he still had time for mischief. He put a turtle in the bath before the monks entered the water, and caused them to run screaming from the bathing area. He mixed ink in the soap, and the harder the monks scrubbed the dirtier they became. After awhile, Koji had caused so much trouble that he was brought to the attention of the Headmaster.

The Headmaster was the most powerful person in the monastery. His word was law. As Koji climbed the steps to his office, he trembled with fear, for he knew that the Headmaster had the power of life and death over him. He knocked softly on the door and was told to enter. As he entered, he bowed low.

Inside, the Headmaster was sitting at a low table, concentrating very hard on reading a scroll. Beside the table there was a large jar, as tall as Koji himself. The jar was filled with candies and as he read the old man reached into the jar and ate the candies.

"I have heard reports about you," the Headmaster said at

last. "You are a prankster. Do you have anything to say for yourself?"

"No, Master," replied Koji.

"I can have you beaten or starved," the Headmaster said. "I can have you put to death, if I choose."

A tear crept out of Koji's eye and rolled slowly off the end of his nose.

"But I will not do these things," said the Headmaster. "I will give you a chance to redeem yourself. Each evening before bed you will clean out the ashes in the large fireplace where the water for the bath is heated. Each morning when you arise you will set the fire before the other boys awaken."

"Thank you, Master," sniffed Koji.

"You may go now," said the Headmaster, and he reached into the jar for a candy.

"What are you eating, Master?" asked Koji.

The Headmaster was shocked at the impertinence of this boy. Moments after being disciplined, he had the nerve to ask such a question. With a twinkle in his eye, he replied, "Koji-chan, this is poison for little boys but good for grown men."

"I understand, Master," said Koji, and with that he left the office.

Days passed and became weeks, and still Koji had to fulfill the duties of his punishment. He didn't complain as he woke early every day to set the fire in the big fireplace, and he didn't cry each evening as he cleaned the ashes of the great cooking fire after all the other boys had gone to bed.

One day, a month after Koji had received his punishment, the Headmaster went on a journey to another monastery. To travel in those days was a very difficult thing. The roads were bad and in some places there were no roads at all. Bandits and thieves lived in the hills and often attacked unsuspecting travellers. To protect him on this journey, the Headmaster took with him one hundred monks. Everyone in the monastery lined up to see them off and wish them a safe trip. Koji, too, lined up with the other boys.

That night, when it was time to go to sleep, Koji said to the other boys, "I know where there is candy."

The other boys laughed. "There is no candy here," said Goki, who was a bully and one of the leaders of the boys.

"I can show you, if you don't believe me," insisted Koji.

"Take us there when everyone is asleep," said Goki. "But I warn you, if this is one of your jokes it will go hard on you."

"You'll see," said Koji. He and the other boys waited until all the monks were asleep. Then they quietly crept out of the room and into the courtyard. The moon was shining and the monastery was bathed in a magical, silvery light. Koji found his way to a set of stairs cut into the wall. This led to the quarters of the senior monks.

"You're not afraid, are you?" laughed Koji when Goki hesitated.

"Keep going," grunted Goki, struggling to hide his nervousness in front of the other boys. And so they climbed the stairs and crept silently along the balcony to where the Headmaster had his rooms. The others hesitated, but Koji laughed. He opened the door and peeked inside.

"Hurry up!" he whispered, motioning to the others to come inside. One by one, they followed him into the room. Moonlight shone through the doorway and Koji could see the low table where the Headmaster had sat just one month ago. Beside the table stood the boy-sized jar of candies, just as it had stood on that day a month ago, filled to the top with candy.

"See," said Koji triumphantly. "I told you that I would find you candies."

"But these candies belong to the Headmaster," objected one boy.

"He will have us killed," said another.

"Or worse!" whined a third.

"Don't worry," laughed Koji. "I'll handle everything. Have you ever seen such candies? Come and eat just one. He'll never miss it." And with that, he popped a candy into his mouth. Then he passed candies to all the other boys.

Soon the boys were taking second and third candies. They had not had sweets for a very long time and they really couldn't help themselves. They ate and ate without stopping, stuffing themselves with the rich food. But even a boy-sized jar has limits, and finally the candies came to an end.

It was then that the boys realized what they had done. They had broken into the Headmaster's office and consumed his entire supply of candy. Perhaps he would not miss one or two or even a dozen candies from such a large jar — but now *all* the candies were gone.

The boys were also feeling another kind of discomfort. After eating so much candy so quickly, they began to have stomachaches.

"Why did we listen to you?" moaned one boy.

"He'll have us beaten, all on account of you," added another.

But Koji just laughed at them. "I'll look after everything," he said. And he went to a shelf on the far wall of the room.

Alone on that shelf was a vase. This was no ordinary vase. It had been brought many years before from China. It was exquisitely made with porcelain so delicate that it was almost transparent, and it had been painted by one of the finest Chinese artists. This vase was the greatest single treasure of the monastery, and all the boys had heard the story of how, long ago, the founder of the order had brought the jar with him from China.

Koji lifted this precious vase above his head and, with one great sweep of his arms, smashed it to the floor beneath his feet. For one long moment, the other boys stared at him in stunned silence. Then they all spoke at once.

"You're crazy!"

"We'll all be killed!"

"Tortured, not killed!"

As the others scurried from the room, Koji laughed again.

From that day on, the boys feared the Headmaster's return. They worked extra hard at their tasks and were careful to obey every order in the hope that, by exemplary behaviour, they could make things right. The monks remarked upon how well-behaved the boys were, and how hard they worked. But inside the Headmaster's office, the boy-sized jar was still empty; and on the Headmaster's floor was a pile of broken china that once had been a priceless vase.

No matter how much an event is hoped for or feared, its time will come, and so the Headmaster returned from his journey. Everyone in the monastery lined up to greet him. The Headmaster and his retinue of one hundred monks swept slowly between the double line of men and boys. They bowed as one, and if you had looked carefully you would have seen the shaking knees of all the boys but one.

The Headmaster strode slowly past the boys, looking neither to the right nor left. He climbed the stairs cut into the wall and walked along the gallery to his rooms. The boys waited, rooted with fear to their spots.

Then, *"Who did this?"* shouted the Headmaster, rushing to the gallery.

"I did, Master," squeaked Koji, stepping out of the line of boys.

"*Come up here!*" ordered the Headmaster. And in front of everyone assembled in the courtyard, Koji slowly made his way up the stairs to the rooms of the Headmaster. The other boys breathed sighs of relief and offered silent prayers that Koji wouldn't reveal their parts in the adventure.

"Tell me how this happened!"

"Well, you see, Master," began Koji, "while you were gone I wanted to thank you for being so lenient with me when I was in trouble. I wondered what I could do for so great a person as you who has everything, and I thought for a very long time. Finally I decided to come up here to your rooms and sweep and dust so that everything would be clean for your arrival. I came with my broom and dustcloths and started to work. As I came to this wall, the end of my broom, which is longer than I am tall, touched the beautiful vase. The vase rocked and then fell, landing as you see it.

"Master, I was told about that vase. I knew that it was the greatest treasure in the Monastery, and I had shattered it. At that moment I wanted to die. I couldn't bear to face your anger. I decided I had to die. I thought of jumping off the balcony, but I might have survived … and then I remembered that you yourself had told me how I might end my worthless life."

"I?" sputtered the Headmaster. "I don't know what you're talking about."

"Yes, Master," Koji continued, "you told me that the candy in the jar was poison for little boys. I remembered and I went to the jar and ate a candy. Nothing happened. I ate more candy, still nothing happened. I ate all the candy but I am still alive."

For a moment, the Headmaster was speechless. Then he

looked at Koji and said, "I am going to teach you a lesson that you will never forget." And with that he closed the door to his rooms.

The other boys and monks strained to hear what went on behind the closed door, but try as they might, they could not hear a word. After a time the stern Headmaster opened the door and Koji reappeared. Silently, he rejoined the boys.

"What happened?" the boys asked, as soon as they had returned to the dormitory. "Did he hit you?" "You don't look hurt." "We thought you were dead."

But Koji didn't reply until all the boys were in bed and the lamps had been put out. Then, in the dark, they heard him whisper, "I bowed to him … and he returned my bow."

And when time had passed and the moment came for the Headmaster to choose his successor, he chose Koji.

▼▼▼▼▼▼

The Orphan Who Became a Great Shaman

Pat Andrews

"I grew up on a trapline, feeling so hungry that when I
got a bowl of porridge one time I just gobbled up the
whole bowlful. But my stomach was so shrunken that
it couldn't hold even a small bowl of porridge. The
porridge came back up. Later I ate slowly one spoonful
of porridge every so often until I had eaten the entire
bowl.

Hunger, cold, loneliness. I grew up snaring rabbits
and catching partridge — doing things that are in the folk
tales I tell. These are the stories that touched on my
childhood, not the stories of kings and queens in castles
waited upon by servants.

I was an adult when I heard my first Inuit folktale.
As the teller unravelled the tale I could feel my fingers
grow cold and my stomach knot with hunger. This was
my world. It was a familiar world. I could close my eyes
and picture the shadows moving on the half-lit cabin
wall. Feel the moan through the place where the moss
chinking had fallen out. Look out the one window and
see the stars, brilliant and plentiful. I remember reading
a folk tale about an Inuit house that had five windows!

Five windows! Can you imagine that! It's unbelievable!

This tale is taken from the *Report of the Canadian Arctic Expedition — 1913-18. The Orphan Who Became a Great Shaman* is a child's dream come true. Here is a boy living alone in the midst of people who treat him shabbily. What happens? Why, as if by magic he is taught to be a Great Shaman. And everyone has to treat him well, now that he is so powerful."

▼▼▼

There was once a small boy whose father was dead. Only his mother was left to look after him, and the other people in the village constantly ill-treated him and made his childhood miserable. Gradually, though, years went by and this small boy grew older and stronger.

One winter, the people in the village built a large dance house where they gathered every evening. The orphan boy still spent nearly all his time in the open air away from the others, however. Even while the others in the village gathered in the dance house, he would wander about outside.

One evening as he roamed outside as usual, the orphan boy saw a brilliant light in the distance. A great desire filled him to find out about the light, so he started walking in its direction. He walked and he walked and he walked. He walked for a very long time.

Finally the boy reached a big dance house. He was gazing through the window when somebody from inside called, "What are you standing out there for? Come in, come inside."

So the boy went inside. He saw men sitting around three sides of the room, so he took his place on the fourth side near the door. Time after time the men asked the boy if he was a shaman, and each time he said, "No, I am not a shaman."

Finally a man sitting on the opposite platform said, "No, you are not a shaman. You are only a poor orphan boy whom everyone ill-treats. I know all about you. That is why I want to help you." Then, getting down from his platform, he turned to another man and said, "Bring me my seal spear and my ice scratcher."

One man went out and brought in the seal spear and the ice scratcher. Then the shaman (for that's who he was) said, "My Spirit. My Spirit, help me. Make ice appear in the floor."

Moments later a tiny circle of ice appeared in the middle of the floor. It gradually widened until it covered the whole space. Then a seal hole opened up in the middle of the ice and a fine fat seal emerged and crawled out on the edge of the ice. The shaman crept up and speared it, cut it up and distributed it among all the people in the dance house. But he did not give any to the boy. Then the ice disappeared and the floor came back. At first the floor was just a little patch in the middle of the ice, but gradually it expanded and superseded the ice. When the floor was in place, the shaman asked the boy if he wished for more, but the boy was too frightened to answer.

"You are a poor boy," the shaman continued, "and I should like to help you very much. Shall I do some more?"

In a barely audible voice the boy managed to whisper, "Yes."

The shaman immediately called out, "My Spirit, my Spirit, help me."

And the floor became covered with newly formed ice pierced with a row of holes through which a fishing net was set. The shaman drew in the net and it was filled with whitefish. He laid the fish out on the ice to freeze. Then he divided them up amongst the people on the platform, just as before. And once again the ice vanished and the house resumed its usual appearance.

Again the shaman called out, "My Spirit. My Spirit, help me."

And this time a moor appeared, with a ring of nooses into which the shaman drove a herd of caribou. When the caribou were all caught, the shaman divided them amongst the people just as he had divided the seal and the fish.

Finally, before daylight, the boy was sent back home.

That evening, all the people in the boy's village gathered at the dance house, and someone said to him, "You! Play something!"

And the boy thought to himself, "Why did everyone over at the other dance house ask me if I was a shaman? I am not a shaman." Then he thought, "But if they are going to call me a shaman, I may as well act like one." So he sat down in the middle of the floor and called, "My Spirit, help me."

Everyone in the boy's village was silent, watching to see what would happen. Presently the floor turned into ice and a seal appeared. The boy speared it and cut it up, and distributed it among the people for them to eat. Similiarly, he obtained whitefish and caribou. And from that time on, all the people of his village respected him, for the orphan boy was now a great shaman.

Name Calling

Itah Sadu

▼▼▼▼▼▼

"One day as I was leaving school, I met a little girl with a sad face standing by the front doors. 'Why are you sad?' I asked. 'Someone called me a name,' she replied. On my way home in the train I created *Name Calling* with the hope that someday, sometime, somewhere, name calling will stop."

▼▼▼

Jennifer called Cindy a name.

Jennifer called Cindy a name, and it hurt bad. It hurt worse than when Cindy had banged her funny bone on the corner of the bed. It hurt worse than when the two-hundred-pound man had stood on her little toe on the train.

Jennifer called Cindy a name and it hurt bad. Jennifer called Cindy a name in the washroom — imagine, the lowest place in the whole school, the place where everybody came to do their business, the place where the public came to do private.

Jennifer called Cindy a name and it hurt bad, so Cindy decided to find Jennifer and make her apologize. And off she went.

The first person Cindy ran into was Karen, and Karen said, "Where are you going in such a rush?" Cindy said, "I'm going to find Jennifer and make her apologize, because in the washroom she hurt my feelings when she called me a name!" And Karen said, "I'll come with you and call her back a name," and off they went.

A little farther off in the corridor they saw Kim, Cindy's best friend, and Kim said, "What's happening? Where's the fire?" Cindy said, "I'm going to find Jennifer and make her apologize, because in the washroom she hurt my feelings when she called me a name, and Karen is coming with me to call her back a name!" And Kim said, "I'll come with you and stomp all over that girl's tongue," and off they went.

As they made their way to the front door, Mark, Cindy's next-door neighbour, came up to them and said, "Excuse me, are we burning rubber or what?" Cindy said, "No, I'm going to find Jennifer and make her apologize, because in the washroom she hurt my feelings when she called me a name, and Karen is coming with me to call her back a name, and Kim is going to stomp all over her tongue!" And Mark said, "Sounds great to me, I'll hold her down," and off they went.

Next to sneak up on them was Oral, the school gossip, the person who minded everybody's business, and he said, "Hey, where are you folks going? Nobody told me about this!" Cindy said, "I'm going to find Jennifer and make her apologize, because in the washroom she hurt my feelings when she called me a name. Karen is coming with me to call her back a name, Kim will stomp all over her tongue and Mark will hold her down!" And Oral said, "I'll come with you and tell the whole school, so they can cheer for you," and off they went.

Just before they got to the front doors, Kate, Cindy's sister, shouted at them, "Is there a party or something? Where's everyone going in such a rush?" Cindy said, "I'm going to find Jennifer and make her apologize, because in the washroom she hurt my feelings when she called me a name. Karen is coming with me to call her back a name, Kim will stomp all over her tongue, Mark will hold her down and Oral will tell everybody in the school so they can cheer for me!" And Kate said, "I'll make sure the fight is fair," and off they went.

At the front doors stood Mr. John, the teacher on hall duty, and Mr. John said, "People, folks, where are you going?" Cindy said, "I'm going to find Jennifer and make her apologize, because in the washroom she hurt my feelings when she called me a name, and Karen is coming with me to call her back a name, Kim will stomp all over her tongue, Mark will hold her down, Oral will tell everybody in the school so they can cheer for me and Kate will make sure we fight fair!" And Mr. John said, "I'll come with you and break up the fight, if it gets started," and off they went.

Outside the school, there was no Jennifer. She was not in the place where she regularly hung out with her friends. So they went to the back of the school, and still there was no Jennifer.

At the back of the school there was no Jennifer, but there was Maxine: Maxine, the one girl in the school nobody smiled with; Maxine, the one girl in the school nobody laughed with; Maxine, the one girl in the school nobody talked to, unless they wanted help with homework. Cindy went up to Maxine and said, "Have you seen Jennifer?" And Maxine said, "No, why are you looking for her?" Cindy said, "She hurt my feelings in the washroom when she called me a name, and Karen is coming with me to call her back a name, Kim will stomp all over her tongue, Mark will hold her down, Oral will tell everybody in the school so they can cheer for me, Kate will make sure we fight fair and Mr. John will break up the fight if it gets started!"

Maxine looked Cindy in the eye and said, "If you don't find Jennifer, will you hate her for the rest of your life?"

Cindy gulped. Then she gulped again. She opened her mouth — nothing came out. Then she rushed back to the group.

Just as Cindy rejoined the group, who should come bopping around the corner of the school but her boyfriend, Mickey B., and he said, "Hey Cindy, are you a rapper or something? Where are you going with all these people?" Cindy said, "I'm going to find Jennifer and make her apologize, because in the washroom she hurt my feelings when she called me a name. And Karen is coming with me to call her back a name, Kim will stomp all over her tongue, Mark will hold her down, Oral will tell everybody in the school so they can cheer for me, Kate will make sure we fight fair and Mr. John will break up the fight if it gets started!" She didn't mention Maxine.

Mickey B. said, "I know where Jennifer is."

"Where's Jennifer?" they all shouted at once.

"She is in the Principal's office," said Mickey B.

"The Principal's office?" they asked. "What's she doing there?"

"Today in math class somebody called her a name and she took them to the Principal's office," said Mickey B., but before the words were out of his mouth everyone rushed past him towards the Principal's office, and as they ran they shouted, "Should I call her a name? Should I stomp on her tongue? Should I hold her down? Should I go and tell everyone? Will you fight fair? Where will you fight?"

When they got to the Principal's office, they heard the sound of someone crying. Cindy stopped and listened. Then she turned to her friends and said, "Thank you. I think I should go into the office alone," and she left the group and went into the office.

The group of friends waited and waited and waited. Finally, the door opened. It was the Principal. She looked at the kids and she looked at Mr. John and then she said, "I think you can all go back to class now." And Mr. John, Mickey B., Kate, Oral, Kim and Karen all walked away down the hall.

They never did find out exactly what happened in the Principal's office. The Principal never told, and Jennifer never told, and Cindy — well, she and Jennifer went back to being friends. But there was some kind of secret between them, a secret that belonged just to them, and they never told anyone else how all that name calling ended.

▼▼▼▼▼▼

Ti-Jean and His
Three Little Pigs

Camille Perron

"After a thirty-two-year career, I retired from teaching in
June 1986. Storytelling in schools, universities, cultural
centres and festivals came to occupy most of my time.
This very enjoyable second career has taken me to
many cities in Ontario, Quebec and even to Whitehorse
in the Yukon. One of my favourites is this tale of *Ti-Jean
and His Three Little Pigs*. It was told to me by Mrs. Eva
Groulx, in March 1937. Her husband Joe had heard it in
the shanties."

▼▼▼

Once upon a time, a long time ago in a country far, far away,
a man, a woman and their son lived in a small house in the
outreaches of the kingdom. They were poor. Their income
came from a small farm near the forest and the meager salary
which the man earned each winter working in bush camps as
a lumberjack.

The boy's name was Ti-Jean. He was eighteen years old
and as curious as a weasel. He wanted to see everything and
he loved girls. Girls were what he was most curious about!

Well, that winter Ti-Jean and his mother stayed home as usual looking after the small stock while the father was gone until late spring to earn a few dollars working in the bush.

Towards the end of winter, on a bright March day, their sow gave birth to three piglets; but these were no ordinary piglets: one was red, one was blue and one was green.

In mid-April, when the camp closed, Ti-Jean's father came back home with the little money he had earned. By the end of May, the money was spent and all they had left to eat were little shrivelled potatoes and turnips.

"Ti-Jean," said the father, "we have not much food left; you will have to go to the city and sell one of our piglets so we can buy something to eat." Well, was Ti-Jean glad! Curious as he was, he would be able to see lots of things ... especially *girls*.

So, the next morning, Ti-Jean got up early, took the little red pig, stuck it in a poke, slapped his cap on his head and left for the city. It was a sunny, bright morning ... the birds were singing, a small breeze caressed his cheeks. Ti-Jean walked merrily, whistling as he went, thinking about what he would see in the city.

Suddenly, about halfway between his home and the town, he saw a cloud of dust rolling down the road in his direction. Just in front of the cloud came a large gold carriage pulled by three teams of pure white thoroughbreds. What a sight! Ti-Jean had never seen anything like it. The horses had their heads tucked in and their ears straight up; their necks were arched and their manes were floating and waving with each step and their tails were lifting and bobbing. Everything on their harnesses sparkled. Ti-Jean had to squint to see them, and his eyes were like buttonholes.

Just as the carriage reached Ti-Jean, "Whoa!" said the driver. The whole thing stopped. The horses bobbed their heads nervously; the cloud of dust settled; the carriage door opened and down came a beautiful young girl. Ti-Jean gasped! The girl smiled and said softly, "Good morning!"

"Good morning," stuttered Ti-Jean.

"Who are you?" asked the girl. "Where are you going?"

"Oh! My name is Ti-Jean. I'm going to the city to sell a little pig."

"A little pig? May I see it?"

"There is no harm in looking," replied Ti-Jean as he swung the sack with the piglet off his shoulder. Then he pulled down the mouth of the bag and the girl peered inside.

"What a beautiful red piglet!" she exclaimed. "Would you give it to me?"

"No!" replied Ti-Jean. "I must go and sell it. We are out of money and have very little to eat."

"Ti-Jean," the girl interrupted, "if you give me your little red piglet, I will show you something that you have never seen before."

Ti-Jean stared at her, hesitated a little and then: "Sure!" he cried. The coachdriver took the poke with the piglet and stuck it in the carriage trunk. The young girl climbed back into the carriage, followed by Ti-Jean. She closed the door and lowered the curtains and then, very deliberately, she lifted the hem of her long skirt, and she lifted her petticoats just a few inches above her delicate ankle and there, halfway up her calf, she had … a mark kind of like a birthmark, like … a sun. Ti-Jean stared. "A sun!!! That's it?" he asked.

"That's it!" she replied.

Disappointed, Ti-Jean went back home and told his father what had happened. "Can't you go and sell a pig by yourself!" cried his father angrily. "Look, Ti-Jean," he continued, "we have no money left; you must go back with another piglet. But this time return with the money!"

"Surely I will!" promised Ti-Jean.

The next morning at daybreak, Ti-Jean took the blue piglet, stuck it in a poke, slapped his cap on his head and left for the city. Again it was one of those beautiful, sunny, bright mornings in May. Ti-Jean was too busy imagining what he would see in the city to notice the birds singing along the roadside and the wind caressing his cheeks. He walked briskly and whistled a merry tune.

Suddenly, when he was about halfway to the city he saw another cloud of dust rolling toward him. In front of it there were the gold carriage and the six beautiful steeds. Ti-Jean's heart pounded like a potato in a wooden shoe. Just as the carriage reached him, "Whoa!" yelled the driver as he pulled on the reins.

Everything came to a dead stop. The cloud of dust settled. The carriage door opened and down came the same beautiful girl Ti-Jean had seen three day before. "Good morning!" she smiled and whispered softly.

"Good morning!" replied Ti-Jean.

"Where are you going this morning, Ti-Jean?"

"Oh! I'm going to the city to sell another piglet."

"Another piglet? May I see it?"

"Oh! There's no harm in looking, is there?"

Ti-Jean rolled the sack with the piglet off his shoulder and opened the mouth of the bag.

"A beautiful blue piglet!" exclaimed the young woman. "I have never seen anything like it! May I have it to keep?"

"Sorry, but no!" replied Ti-Jean. "I must sell it! My father would be very upset if I just gave it away. We have no more money and very little food."

"Ti-Jean," she said, "if you give me your little blue piglet, I will show you something else that you have never seen before."

Ti-Jean, curious as he was, looked at the girl hesitantly.

"Oh! … Well! … Fine!" he said finally, and he handed the poke with the piglet to the coachdriver, who stuck it in the carriage trunk.

The young girl climbed into the carriage with Ti-Jean. She shut the door, closed the curtains, smiled at Ti-Jean, lifted the hem of her skirt, lifted her petticoats past the ankle, above the sun, right up to just above her knee where she had another mark, a birthmark … like a moon.

"A moon? … A moon!" exclaimed Ti-Jean. "Is that it?" he whispered, blinking at the beautiful moon.

"That's it!"

Ti-Jean returned home and tried to explain to his father what had happened.

"Ti-Jean!" cut in his father. "You have the brains of a mop! A man of your age who can't even sell a pig!!! Look, my boy! We have but one little pig left. If you give this one away we will have to survive the rest of the summer eating little dried up potatoes and turnips. Do you think you can go out and sell this last piglet and bring me back the money?"

"Yes, of course!" said Ti-Jean. "I won't be taken in this time."

The next morning, Ti-Jean got up with the sun. Again it was one of those beautiful mornings in May. Ti-Jean put the green piglet into a poke, swung the poke on his shoulder, slapped on his cap and started walking briskly towards the city. He could feel the warm rays of the sun on his back and the piglet grunting contentedly in its sack. Again Ti-Jean was daydreaming about what he might see when he reached town. And again, about halfway into town, he saw a familiar cloud of dust rolling in his direction. The wheels of the golden carriage were turning so fast that the spokes were like twirling sunrays. The three teams of white thoroughbreds pranced prettily towards him.

Well, Ti-Jean, who was well aware of his weakness, looked briefly at the carriage and then turned his back to the road.

"Whoa!" cried the driver, and the carriage rolled to a stop.

Ti-Jean glanced briefly over his shoulder and saw the beautiful lady opening the carriage door.

"Good morning, Ti-Jean," she said softly.

Ti-Jean's knees turned to jelly. "Good morning," he said roughly, over his shoulder.

"Where are you going this morning?" the girl continued, as if Ti-Jean had been as friendly as ever.

"To town! To sell a pig."

"A pig? Another piglet? May I see it?"

"No!" said Ti-Jean emphatically.

"Ti-Jean, just a brief look?" she teased, winking at him as he looked at her from over his shoulder.

"Just a peek!" he warned as he swung the poke in an arc off his shoulder and placed it gently on the ground. He opened the bag and her eyes widened at the sight of the little green pig.

"Oh! Ti-Jean!" she exclaimed. "What a beautiful little piglet! This one is surely my favourite. Ti-Jean," she begged, "can I have it?"

"No!!!"

"Ti-Jean, please, puh-lease! Tell you what. If you give me your little green piglet, I will show you something you have never seen before, something I have never shown to anyone else, something that no one else, no one but you alone, shall ever see …"

"Ah, no …" Ti-Jean hesitated. "No one?" he questioned.

"No one!" she smiled back.

"Well … Okay," said Ti-Jean, as he gave the poke and the pig to the coachdriver, who in turn placed it in the carriage trunk.

The beautiful girl climbed aboard the carriage with Ti-Jean on her heels. She shut the door, she closed the curtains, and, blushing, she lifted up her skirts and her petticoats and her crinolines. She passed the sun, she passed the moon, and up, way up on her thigh, she had a mark like a birthmark, like a cluster of stars. Ti-Jean's eyes nearly popped out of their sockets; his fingers twitched; he gasped in surprise; his mouth dropped open. "Ohooooh!" murmured Ti-Jean. And, after a moment of silence ... "Is that it?" he asked.

"That's it," she replied.

Well, Ti-Jean went back home. His father was waiting. Ti-Jean confessed his failure. His father's face turned a ghastly white, with red blotches.

"To the woodshed!" he ordered Ti-Jean, as he pointed in the direction of the small building. Well, you can imagine that once his father had finished, Ti-Jean had a sore seat. He couldn't sit down for three days.

"You have spider webs for a brain," said Ti-Jean's father. "You gave away all our piglets. We have no money, and nothing to eat but shrivelled up and dried little potatoes and turnips ... and it's your fault!"

"Well, what is done is done," replied Ti-Jean, "and I cannot undo it."

"It's going to be a long, long summer," murmured Ti-Jean to himself.

Meanwhile, at the King's castle in the city, the Monarch decided that his young Princess, who was precisely Ti-Jean's age, was old enough to be married. She was such a beauty that all the noblemen who had laid eyes on her wanted her as their wife. Not knowing which husband to choose for her, the King decided that she would marry the man who could guess her deepest secret, for he was sure that only a very, very special man would be able to guess what secret she held. So the King wrote a proclamation on a large piece of parchment and he sent his criers to all the surrounding kingdoms and to all the cities of his kingdom. The town criers went out into all the public squares and rang out:

"A proclamation of his Majesty the King. Whosoever shall guess the secret of my daughter, the Princess, shall have her hand in marriage and half of my kingdom. Signed by the King."

Well, you should have seen what happened. From all the surrounding kingdoms and from all the major cities far and wide they came: unmarried kings and princes and dukes, and barons and marquis and even knights; from all the high and low nobility they came, to try and guess the Princess's secret. On their great steeds they came, with their richest apparel, and most luxurious gifts. The suitors lined up along the inner wall waiting for their turn to see the Princess and venture their guess as to what her secret might be. But not one of them knew.

Meanwhile, Ti-Jean was at home with his parents. One day he heard about the King's proclamation.

"Poppa! Momma! I know the Princess's secret!" said Ti-Jean excitedly.

"Ti-Jean," grumbled his father, "calm your nerves."

"I know it and I'm going."

"Ti-Jean! Let me explain. You are a peasant boy. We are poor, of the lowest class. The Princess is rich and she is of nobility. A rich noble Princess does not marry a poor peasant boy like you."

"I know her secret and I'm going," repeated Ti-Jean obstinately.

"They'll mock you and laugh at you, my poor boy," lamented his mother.

"It doesn't matter! I'm going!"

"If you go and get scorned, don't you come and cry on our shoulders," said Ti-Jean's father.

Ti-Jean slapped on his cap and ran to the castle to line up with the others. Well, when they saw Ti-Jean, they turned up their noses, passed ahead of him and said: "Ti-Jean, you're poor! You have no business here; go home!" Or: "Ti-Jean, you're from the lowest class; you're a lumberjack's son. You shouldn't be here — go home!" Or: "Ti-Jean, you stink! You smell like a pig! Go home!"

But Ti-Jean stayed and stayed and stayed. All the others passed ahead of him but he never complained and never said anything; he just waited, and waited and waited. Three nights and three days he waited.

Finally, there was no one else left in the courtyard. All but Ti-Jean had gone in and had left disappointed. The King came out on the balcony of the castle. He leaned on the railing and yelled: "Anyone else?"

"No one, your Majesty," replied the King's men.

"There's me!" cried out Ti-Jean, waving his cap to the King.

"He doesn't count, your Majesty," said the King's men. "He is poor, from the lowest class, a peasant's son, a lumber-jack."

"Well, give me a chance!" yelled out Ti-Jean. "Just be-cause my father is poor and just because we don't have a beautiful house and important jobs, we are worth as much as anybody else. Isn't that right, your Majesty?" The King was taken by surprise. He was King for all his subjects. He had to appear just.

"Ah, let him in! Perhaps we shall be amused. Ha! Ha! Ha!" laughed the King as he went back to his throne.

When Ti-Jean entered, he saw the King sitting solemnly by the Queen, who was also wearing her crown. And standing

there, between her parents, was the beautiful girl that Ti-Jean
had seen in the carriage. She smiled and winked at him, for
she liked this Ti-Jean and his little pigs.

"Well, my lad," queried the King, "what is the secret of my
daughter, the Princess?"

Ti-Jean, who was polite and well-reared, removed his cap,
bowed gracefully before the King and Queen, and said in a
clear voice: "With all due respect, your Majesty, Sire, my King,
your daughter has a sun, a moon and a cluster of stars," and
as he spoke, Ti-Jean pointed to his lower leg, his calf, and
finally slapped his thigh.

The King's eyes rolled and he fainted; he fell right off his
throne. His crown rolled all the way to the feet of Ti-Jean,
who picked it up and placed it on his head. Then the Queen
fainted, but the Princess smiled at Ti-Jean and danced excitedly.

Well, three days later, Ti-Jean and the Princess were
married.

Ti-Jean moved his father and mother to the castle. They
didn't have to eat little shrivelled potatoes and turnips all
summer, oh no!

They raised many, many children, Ti-Jean and his Princess, and one day, as they were walking in the garden, Ti-Jean
stepped on a mouse's tail and it said, "cui, cui, that's the end
of my tale."

The Mysterious Singing Drum
Bob Barton

"This is the first story I ever learned, many years ago.
I memorized it verbatim from Kathleen Arnott's
African Myths and Legends. I told it to hundreds of
children over a period of fifteen years. Then recently I
re-read the original text and was shocked to find I had
unconsciously made the story entirely my own.
Although we don't know the name of the African
storyteller who first gave it to be written down, the
story is from Bantu oral tradition."

Long ago, in an African village by the sea, there lived a little
girl who loved to collect shells. She collected cowries and
scallops, snails and periwinkles, multi-coloured top shells
and red-rayed keyhole limpets. She was very proud of her
collection and could hardly wait to finish her chores each day
so that she could rush to the water's edge to search among
the rocks and in the tide pools.

One night there was a fierce storm. Waves pounded the
shoreline and wind wailed through the tree tops, but none of
this frightened the little girl. Instead she was so excited that

she couldn't sleep, for she knew that in the morning the beach would be strewn with all kinds of treasures from the sea.

The little girl was not disappointed. Next morning after chores, she and the other village children made their way to the seashore. As far as they could see, the beach was awash with sea plants and creatures, driftwood, pebbles and shells.

The children began sifting and sorting among the rocks and pools and sand. All at once the little girl cried out, "Everyone! Come, see what I've found!" The others dropped what they were doing and came to the little girl's side.

In her hand she was holding a tiny white shell. It was not a particularly interesting shell. Its shape was quite ordinary and it bore no special markings. The other children began to grumble and complain.

"Why did you call us over? That shell is worthless!" They began to leave when the little girl cried, "Watch this!" They turned. The little girl had closed her fingers over the shell.

"Think of a colour," she demanded.

"Purple," replied the boy closest to her.

The little girl uncurled her fingers. The shell had turned purple. She cupped her other hand over the shell and called out, "Another colour!"

"Pink," shouted a girl.

The little girl took away her hand and in her outstretched palm the shell glowed a pale pretty pink.

Once again she covered the shell with her other hand and called for another colour.

The children crowded around. "Green."

"Tangerine."

"Turquoise."

"Violet," they hollered. They were rewarded each time with the colour of their choice. It was as if every colour of the rainbow was in that shell.

Now all of the children were determined that they were going to find a shell just like the little girl's and they scattered along the water's edge.

The little girl did not want to cease exploring the seashore but she was concerned about the safekeeping of her precious shell. She had no pockets, nor was she carrying any sort of container. Then she had an idea. Behind her were low rocky cliffs. She climbed up the rocks and placed her shell in an indentation near the top of the cliff. Then she climbed down and ran off to join the other children.

That day, the children enjoyed themselves so much that they completely lost track of the time. Suddenly one boy noticed how low the sun had dipped in the sky. "The sun is setting," he shouted. "Come everyone, we've got to hurry home!" Clutching their findings, the children started to run. "Wait!" cried a voice. They turned. It was the little girl.

"We can't go home yet," she explained. "I've left my shell way down the beach on the cliffs."

"It will soon be dark," said one of the older children. "You can't go back now."

"Besides, we're tired and hungry and everyone will be worried about us," said another.

"I've got it," said the boy who was leading them. "We'll come back first thing in the morning."

"Yes," said another girl. "Your shell will be quite safe where you left it until then."

"I'm not setting foot from here until I get my shell," said the little girl and she planted her feet firmly in the sand.

"Well," they said, "fetch it yourself. We're leaving!" And they all ran off.

The little girl stood watching them, then she turned and plodded back towards the rocky cliffs. The sun was sliding beneath the horizon and clouds of dusk were gathering. For the first time, the little girl began to feel scared.

"Eeeeee … AHHHH!" She heard a distant groaning sound, like a huge creature trapped in a cave and she stopped dead in her tracks.

What had made that sound? "Oh, it's only my imagination playing tricks on me," thought the little girl. "It's probably nothing more than the sound of the wind whistling through the rocks just ahead!" But there was no wind. There was scarcely a breeze.

The girl thought, "I'll sing to myself. That always helps when I'm scared."

She continued walking, but now she sang at the top of her lungs:

"My shell
My shell
Bone white in the sand.
My shell
My shell
Rainbow in my hand."

The sun had disappeared now; darkness was closing in. The little girl halted and squinted into the gathering gloom. She was certain she had seen something move near the cliffs where she had left her shell.

"I've got to stop imagining things," she whispered. "I'm scaring myself half to death!" She sang even louder now.

"My shell
My shell
Bone white in the …"

Suddenly she looked up. The song died in her throat.

Sitting atop the rock where she had left her shell was the most enormous, ugly ogre she had ever seen in her life. He peered at her through bloodshot eyes and smiled with a mouthful of cracked and broken teeth.

"Come closer, little girl, and sing that song again to me!" he thundered.

The little girl's knees turned to jelly and her heart hammered in her throat but she managed somehow to squeak out the song.

"My shell
My shell
Bone white in the sand.
My shell
My shell
Rainbow in my hand."

When she had finished, the ogre said, "Sing it one more time. I like that song!" The little girl sang a second time. The ogre leaned towards her and croaked, "Come closer, little girl, and I'll give you your shell!" The little girl approached the ogre, who held out her shell in his hairy, stubby fingers. As she reached for the shell, the ogre grabbed her by the wrist, tossed the shell over his shoulder, and cried, "Aha, now I've got you, haven't I?" The ogre reached behind the rocks and produced a large zebra-striped, wooden drum. Then he removed the drum-skin from the top of the drum and put the little girl inside. After replacing the drum-skin, he held the drum up in front of him and shouted to the little girl, "Now, my little one, whenever I play my drum, you must sing for me and if you don't sing, I'll eat you!" Then he shouldered the drum, clambered down from the rocky cliff, and flip-flopped his way into the night.

The ogre hadn't eaten for a long time. Maybe his singing drum could get him the meal he longed for — boiled chicken and homebrewed beer.

Just ahead at the edge of the jungle was the village.

The flip-flop sounds of the approaching ogre were heard by the villagers. Frantically they dashed to find hiding places, for it was well known that ogres could do terrible damage to a village. They stepped on dogs and knocked over houses. The villagers weren't about to take any chances.

By the time the ogre squatted down in the centre of the village, no one was visible. The ogre decided to charm them with his music. He tapped out a gentle rhythm on the drum and the little girl inside the drum began to sing.

"My shell
My shell …"

Suddenly he stopped and cried out, "Villagers, bring me boiled chicken and homebrewed beer and I'll play my magic drum for you."

Some of the villagers began to edge forward from their hiding places, eager to see this wondrous instrument. Some of them uttered excitedly, "The ogre appears to speak the truth. Surely this is indeed a magic instrument."

Then a frantic whisper silenced them. "That's no magic drum! That's my daughter's voice. The ogre has kidnapped her!" It was the little girl's mother speaking. The villagers pressed about the girl's mother, trying to figure out how to get the child away from the ogre.

"Let's get our spears and rush him," whispered one reckless fellow. "He'll not be able to defend himself against all of us."

"Too risky," offered another. "I say we lure him under the trees and drop our fishing nets over him. Then we'll tie him up and drag him into the sea."

"You're not using your heads," hissed one of the elders. "Ogres are said to possess magical powers. Why, this one is likely to turn us into gourds or something much worse if we're not careful."

"I've got it," said another voice. "He calls for boiled chicken and homebrewed beer. Let's give it to him until he's stuffed. Perhaps then he'll fall asleep and we can snatch the child and run for it!"

"That's it, then!" said the villagers, and within minutes they were scurrying about the village heaping platters with boiled chicken and filling calabashes with homebrewed beer.

The villagers placed the food and drink before the ogre. He guzzled the beer, stuffed his face with boiled chicken and gobbled everything so greedily that he chewed the third finger of his right hand along with the chicken. The calabashes were quickly drained and the platters cleaned. Then the ogre gave a mighty belch and raised his great hairy arms in the air above the drum.

Before he could strike a note, however, his head rolled forward on his chest, he yawned, and his arms and body slumped over the drum. A loud snore burst from his mouth.

The little girl's mother leapt forward with a knife between her teeth. She motioned the others to keep still and then she bellied her way up to the drum. Ever so slowly she reached out and eased the ogre's hairy arms from the surface of the drum. Next she tilted the drum towards her slightly, took the knife from her teeth, and carefully slit the drum's skin around the edge. She rolled the drum-skin back and peered in. It was indeed her daughter in the drum, a bit cramped but otherwise unharmed. The mother lifted her daughter out gently and carried her safely to the other villagers.

Then the mother called for three work parties. To the first she instructed, "Go quickly into the jungle and capture two poisonous snakes. Bring them back alive!"

To the second party she said, "We will need a hive of stinging bees. Use smoke to drive them from their nest."

To the third party she ordered, "Collect biting ants from

rotting tree trunks. Bring back only those that are as big as your thumbs." While the volunteers fanned out into the jungle, the others kept a nervous watch over the ogre.

When the wriggling, twisting snakes were fetched, the mother ordered them stuffed into the ogre's drum. Next were the bees, drugged from their smoky capture. Finally, the biting thumb-sized ants went into the drum.

The drum-skin was quickly stretched over the open drum and stitched into place. Then the villagers hid again and watched and waited.

In the early hours of the morning, just before dawn, a low rumbling was heard. Thinking it the sound of thunder, the villagers gazed skywards. The moon still glowed brightly and the stars were clearly visible. Then they realized that what they thought was the sound of thunder was actually the ogre's belly rumbling. He woke with a start, hungry.

He struck the drum sharply on the side, and whispered harshly, "Psst, little girl, wake up, I'm hungry; I need you to sing," and he cried out to the villagers for food, promising to entertain them again with his playing. But as he struck a lively rhythm on the drum-skin, no sweet-voiced child accompanied him.

He stopped playing and croaked fiercely to the drum, "Wake up, little girl, now!" Again he played. Again no voice accompanied him.

The ogre was about to rip the skin from the top of the drum when he remembered that the villagers were probably watching him from behind rocks and walls and bushes and trees. Not about to reveal his secret to anyone, he hauled himself to his feet and flip-flopped into the jungle with the drum clutched to his chest.

The villagers followed him with their eyes as long as they were able and then they waited.

When he had gone far from the village, the ogre angrily tore the skin from the drum. The foul-tempered bees, recovered from their smoky stupor, instantly flew at the ogre's head. The thumb-sized ants swarmed over his body, and the poisonous snakes curled themselves around his limbs. The ogre had to use all his powers to escape the deadly attack. With magic, he changed his shape, and felt the damp jungle soil close around him.

Meanwhile, the impatient villagers listened for the ogre's dying shrieks. But it was strangely quiet in the jungle.

Finally they made their move. Arming themselves with their knives, they plunged forward through the long grasses and among the trees.

Suddenly, they saw the drum. The top had been ripped off. The ants were gone, the bees were gone, the snakes were gone, and the ogre was gone.

His body was nowhere in sight.

The villagers beat the bushes in the immediate vicinity. How could this be? How could the ogre vanish into thin air?

Suddenly, a blood-curdling scream pierced the air.

Everyone whirled around. Standing beside the drum, frantically clutching at her lower leg, was the little girl's mother. Long snakelike tendrils of a human-eating plant had coiled around the mother's leg. The vile plant was slowly dragging her towards the spiky mouth at its centre.

The villagers sprang to her assistance. They linked their arms around each other's waists, forming a human chain. Then they grasped the waist of the little girl's mother and a fierce tug of war ensued.

With an incredible pull, the villagers finally snapped the tendril attached to the mother and fell backwards in a great heap. As they struggled to their feet, the plant's other tendrils snaked out in their direction.

Everyone fled, and from that day until this, no one has ventured near that part of the jungle and nor has the ogre been heard of again.

Perhaps the plant still grows in that distant jungle.

Perhaps the shell that started the whole adventure waits on some sandy seashore for another child to find it and sing ...

"My shell
My shell
Bone white in the sand.
My shell
My shell
Rainbow in my hand."

Tricksters

▼▼▼▼▼▼▼

Voiceover

The next time a bully has you cornered and you can't outrun, outspend or outbash him, remember what these stories say: bullies are stupid. If you can't outbully them, try doing what Jack Fury, Renato the Italian cook, and Chanticleer the rooster do: Use your wits. And if that doesn't work, develop your pitching arm — it helped Lynda Howes deal with a serious raccoon problem.

Native storytellers tell of another kind of trickster. My old friend Angela Sidney, who died in 1981, used to sit by the river in Whitehorse, Yukon Territory, and relate how Crow made the world: Crow stole the light from a rich chief who was hoarding it; Crow stole sand from a greedy chief when the earth was covered with water. "Become a world!" Crow cried, casting the sand forth upon the water to create the land we tread upon, under the light of the Crow-stolen sun, moon and stars. What this most generous and mischievous of tricksters stole, he/she gave away again to the humans and animals.

Angela was Tagish-Tlingit, and her name for Trickster was Crow. In this section, you'll meet Trickster in the Ojibway tradition of Gilbert Oskaboose and Lenore Keeshig-Tobias. These tales remind us of the Creator's great and paradoxical lesson: The world belongs to you; the world does not belong to you. The world is Trickster's astonishing gift to those who dwell upon it.

Reynard and Chanticleer

Melanie Ray

"'Fox went out on a chilly night/Prayed to the moon to
give him light …' A song still sung today about one of
the most durable of rascals, Reynard the Fox. He's all
over the place causing trouble, and mostly getting away
with it. He pops up in England flinging ducks across his
back; he tricks a Russian King into giving wealth and a
daughter to a peasant; he makes the more dull-witted
wolf sorry he ever met him, and he charms birds out of
the trees by playing dead. (Real foxes have done that,
by the way.) And once in a great while, he is himself
'outfoxed.'

I found this story in *Reynard the Fox*, Kenneth
Varty's scholarly study of this trickster in English folklore.
It was from a French epic poem written by Pierre St.
Cloud in 1175 A.D., with traceable roots going back to
Roman times. I also read the more famous version by
Chaucer in his *Canterbury Tales*. Then I started telling it,
until it grew into the story you will read here."

This was to be Reynard's lucky day! All summer long, that
clever fox had prowled around Farmer Constant's barnyard,

looking for a way in to the hens, with no luck. But today, today, one nail in one board in the fence was a little bit loose! He pulled and pried, and chewed and pushed and, at last, squeezed through.

Huge green cabbages grew in this corner of the yard, and Reynard ducked beneath the nearest leaves. Then from cabbage to cabbage he crawled on his belly toward the hens, the fine fat hens, who were too busy eating grubs to notice their danger.

But Pertelote, fluffy Pertelote, white Pertelote, the queen of the barnyard and the smartest of the hens, caught sight of the trembling of a cabbage leaf when there was no wind, the flash of a red brush in the sun.

"Fox!" she cried, and she began to run.

"Fox!" cried all the other hens and they ran after her.

She ran for the compost pile, where her husband Chanticleer the rooster was standing guard.

"Fox! Did you see him? There's a fox in the cabbages! A fox! Warn the goodwife!" But the truth of it was, Chanticleer had seen nothing. Chanticleer had been dozing in the hot sun. But he was not going to tell his wife that, no, no, no. Quickly he looked round, and of course did not see the fox, for Reynard was keeping very still in the cabbage shadows.

"Nonsense," he said. "I would have seen a fox in the yard from here."

They squawked at each other, but in the end, Pertelote, with all her sisters, left him. They went under the hazelnut trees, as far away as they could get from the cabbage patch.

Chanticleer looked about him. Everything lay still under the sun — especially Reynard.

"Obviously no fox," Chanticleer said to himself. The sun warmed his feathers, the bees droned over the marigolds, and Chanticleer grew drowsy with the heat. He slept again, but his time he had a dream.

In his dream, a great shadowy beast he could not see tried to wrap a smelly red fur coat around him. A red fur coat with a bone collar. The beast was trying to close it round Chanticleer's neck. Tighter … tighter … tighter …

"Pertelote! Pertelote!"

Reynard lay still. Pertelote came running. Chanticleer told her his dream. Reynard listened, and he had to hold his ribs tight to keep his laughter from shaking the cabbage he was under. Pertelote listened, but she did not laugh.

"A red fur coat — that is the fox!" she said. "And the collar, the bone collar, it is his teeth! Oh, my husband, the fox is going to get you by the neck!" Pertelote began to weep and flutter about the compost pile.

Chanticleer was frightened, but he could not let his wife know that, no, no, no. So he said, "My, my, you seem to have foxes on the brain. It was just a dream, a silly dream."

At last he persuaded Pertelote to go back to the other hens and only then did he look again at the shadows beneath the cabbages. There was nothing to see, Reynard made sure of that! He thought he would crow, to cheer himself up. He raised his head, shut his eyes, and gave a mighty crow. "CO-KI-O-CO!"

When he looked down again, there was the fox, sitting at the foot of the compost pile, smiling at Chanticleer with all his white, fascinating teeth.

"What a beautiful voice you have, Chanticleer," said Reynard. "Do you know I can hear you twenty fields away? Do you know that I have come just to listen to you sing? Please, sing for me again."

Chanticleer thought, "Sing for a fox?! He must think I am very stupid indeed! No, no, no, no, no!" He would not!

But Reynard continued in this honeyed vein, and at last Chanticleer thought that it would do no harm to sing, as long as he kept his eyes on the fox. So Chanticleer raised his head, looked down his beak at Reynard with both eyes (which is hard to do if you are a rooster), and sang, "Co-ki-o-co."

"Lovely!" said Reynard. "You are going to be better than your father, Chanticleer, and oh, how I enjoyed your father! But do you know, he had a little trick. He always used to close his eyes to clarify the top notes. You should try it." Chanticleer thought, "Close my eyes in front of a fox! He must think I am one very dumb cluck! No, no, no, no, no! I will not do that!"

But Reynard pleaded and flattered, and at last Chanticleer thought that there could be no harm if he closed just one eye ... So he raised his head, looked down his beak with one eye, and sang, "Co-ki-o-co."

"Bravo! That's more like it." Reynard's tail twitched with excitement. "But I do think that top note was still a teeny bit flat. What do you think — "

Chanticleer did not think at all. He raised his head, he opened his beak, he closed both eyes — and Reynard leapt up the compost pile, clamped his teeth around Chanticleer's neck, threw him over his back and set off running for the gap in the fence.

Pertelote saw him.

"Fox!" she cried, and all the hens joined in. "Fox! Fox!"

This got all the other barnyard animals mooing and braying and squealing and bleating, "Fox! Fox!"

The farmer's wife heard all the noise and came out of the kitchen in time to see the fox's tail disappear through the fence.

"Fox!" she screamed, and beat on her pot with a wooden spoon. Her husband, Farmer Constant, came running from the barn and saw the fox streaking through the corn with his prize rooster!

"Fox!" he cried. "Help, ho! Bring on the dogs!"

Farmers and dogs came running from everywhere. They chased Reynard across the fields, cursing and howling at him every step of the way. But Reynard, even with a fine plump rooster on his back, was very fast. Long before the hounds could catch him, he had reached the shelter of the forest.

As the shadows deepened around them, and the sounds of the chase receded, Chanticleer knew that no one but he could save himself from becoming a chicken dinner.

"Reynard," he croaked. (It was hard for him to speak because Reynard had him by the throat.) "Listen to what those louts are calling you! Such bad names! How can you let them get away with that! Why do you not shout back defiance? Tell them I am yours no matter what they do!"

Well! No one is so clever that they cannot be tricked once. Reynard listened to Chanticleer, and the next time he heard a farmer call out, "Stop, you red-haired thief!" he opened his mouth to reply, and like that Chanticleer was flapping his wings as fast as he could. He flew to the top of a tree, and called out to Reynard, pacing below.

"So, Reynard, what do you think of this?"

Reynard snarled up at him, "Cursed be the mouth that opens when it should stay shut!"

"Yes," said Chanticleer, "you could look at it that way. But my wife now, Pertelote, she would look at it another way. She would say, and I have to agree, 'Cursed be the eyes that shut when they should stay open!' CO-KI-O-CO!"

Jack Fury

Joe Neil MacNeil
(translated from Gaelic
by John Shaw)

"'What the ear does not hear will not move the heart.'
This is a saying from Cape Breton storyteller Joe Neil
MacNeil. Now in his eighties, Joe Neil is considered to
be one of the finest storytellers in the Scottish Gaelic
tradition. He began listening to the tellers of his
neighbourhood when he was a young boy, and has
kept those stories with him all of his life. He grew up in
a time when people were not devoted to radio and
television, and had plenty of time for talking and
remembering stories. In a wonderful book of
reminiscences and stories he made with folklorist
John Shaw —*Tales Until Dawn*— Joe Neil recalls
that, 'Generally the long tales were the ones that
most pleased people. It did not matter whether it was
a man or a woman who was a good storyteller. When
she or he began, the tale was so enjoyable and would
please you so well as it progressed that you would find
yourself hoping that it would not end for a long time,
that there would be a great amount of working around
it so that the storyteller could make it very, very long

until the end of the tale. You would have some idea of what was going to happen, but it was as if you did not understand and you were only seeing in your mind how the story was unfolding and you didn't think about how it was going to end at all.'

Joe Neil learned the story of *Jack Fury* from a storyteller named John MacIsaac. Joe Neil says that when John told about a character in a tale, 'You would think that he was that man and that the story was happening right in front of him.'

This version of *Jack Fury* includes some minor changes from John Shaw's original translation. These changes were made with the translator's permission."

— *D.Y.*

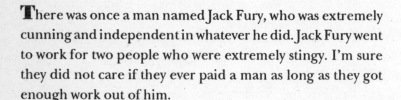

There was once a man named Jack Fury, who was extremely cunning and independent in whatever he did. Jack Fury went to work for two people who were extremely stingy. I'm sure they did not care if they ever paid a man as long as they got enough work out of him.

Anyway, Jack Fury went to work for the two stingy people, plowing a field with oxen. He was a strong man and quick-tempered, and as he was going around with the oxen a bird alighted and started to sing in a tree. Jack Fury thought that somebody was making fun of him and he decided that it was the bird. So he picked up a large stone to throw at the bird — and what did he do but strike one of the oxen, and the ox fell over dead. There was no help for it, so he continued plowing with the other one. Then he skinned the dead ox, and in the evening he took the oxhide with him to town.

NEXT TELLER

He arrived at a certain place in the town, and where was that but the shoemaker's. He was thinking that perhaps the shoemaker would need leather and would buy the oxhide and get it tanned. But when he arrived, it seems that the shoemaker was away and that a gentleman was with the shoemaker's wife. So Jack Fury said to the gentleman, "Well, you have been caught in a compromising situation and it will not go so easily for you as you might expect when I see your host and tell him."

The gentleman replied, "Please, don't say anything. I will give you five English pounds to keep quiet."

"Oh," he replied, "five English pounds! What is five English pounds to me? Don't you know that I am not going to conceal this matter for a trifling sum of money?"

"In that case," said the gentleman, "I will give you ten English pounds."

"I'll have nothing to do with it," said Jack Fury. "I am not going to let this matter concerning my good friend pass for such a trifling sum of money."

"I'll give you twenty pounds," said the gentleman, "just for keeping quiet."

"Well, then," Jack Fury replied, "I would not mind being quiet, since you are so concerned about my remaining so." So he got twenty English pounds for the oxhide.

Later that evening when he reached home, Jack Fury's two bosses asked him how he had got along, and he said that he did not get along very well at all, although he had begun well enough. But some creature had made fun of him while he was plowing and he threw a pebble at it in order to drive it away or kill it. "And," said Jack Fury, "I struck one of the oxen and I killed it."

Well, believe me, Jack Fury's bosses were angry then. He continued, "I skinned the ox and I took the hide with me and went to town and shouted to see if there was anyone who would buy an oxhide, and they bought the oxhide from me."

"And what did you get?" they asked.

"I got twenty pounds for it."

"And do you think if we took the hide of the other ox in, that they would buy it?"

"Oh, I don't know," said he, "but I think that if I had had a number of oxhides with me, I could have sold them."

So the two bosses killed the other ox and went to town, calling out, "Who will buy an oxhide?" And the townspeople thought they were so foolish that they started after the bosses with their dogs and drove them all the way home.

The two stingy bosses were angry when they arrived back, but I am sure that they did not show many signs of it. But Jack Fury was canny, so he listened behind their door to find out how things were going, and heard them planning to do away with him that night as he slept in his bed.

Now, there were two old ladies in the household, two old housekeepers. And Jack Fury went over to one of them — he was almost crying — and he said to her, "I have bad news for you. They are talking about doing away with you tonight. But," he said, "if you come over and sleep in the bed where I am sleeping now, you will be safe enough."

And the old woman believed him and came over and slept in his bed, and he went and slept in hers. And that night the bosses came and killed the old woman.

When Jack arose in the morning, his bosses stared at him. "And what," said they, "brought you here?"

"And why," said he, "shouldn't I be here?"

"And where did you sleep last night?"

"I slept in the bed over there," said he. "The old lady came to me complaining that she was not getting enough sleep, and I said to her that she would be better off sleeping in my bed, my bed was quite good and I would go over to the old lady's bed. And I slept well enough in her bed. And I found nothing wrong with it."

Oh, that made Jack Fury's bosses angry, but they did not let on at all. They said to him, "Now you must go and bury the old lady."

"Oh," replied Jack, "I will not go with her today. You must give me time. I will go with her tomorrow morning."

And so it came to pass that Jack Fury set out the next morning and he took the old woman's body with him, and a basket on his arm. He travelled with the basket and the old lady in tow and he reached his destination just as the day broke. He reached the place of a rich gentleman, and he left the old woman standing up at the well with the basket on her arm. Then he went up, knocked on the door, and complained to the rich gentleman. He said that he and his mother were so poor in the world that they were travelling around with a basket of eggs to see if they could sell them and get some food to eat. The gentleman said, "Tell her to come down."

"She won't come down," Jack Fury replied. "She has given out. She is so tired that she can't come down. She has given up walking, and I'm tired myself."

"Well, then," said the gentleman, "I will send down a servant to talk to her and ask her to come down, so that you will get food until I buy the eggs from you."

And Jack Fury said to the rich man's servant: "Now," said he, "my mother is very deaf and you may have to give her a slight push to make sure that she hears and realizes you are speaking to her."

So down went the gentleman's manservant, and when he reached the old woman he spoke to her and shouted to her, but she did not answer; so he gave her a slight push and she fell into the well. And Jack started weeping and lamenting.

"You have killed my mother," said he. "And how am I going to stand being so destitute in this world without my mother?"

"Oh, take it easy, take it easy," said the gentleman.

"It is easy enough for you, my fine fellow, to say that. But as for me, I have lost my mother."

"Listen," said the gentleman, "take it easy there."

"Oh," Jack Fury replied, "I will do nothing of the sort. I am going to take this matter to the law. Your servant pushed my mother into the well without just cause and she was drowned. And I am going to take that to the law."

"Oh, take it easy," said the gentleman. "Take it easy. I will give you a settlement."

"Money means nothing to me," said Jack. "What good will your money do me compared to my mother?"

"Now," said the gentleman, "I will give you ten English pounds to keep quiet about the matter."

"Ten English pounds for my mother!" said Jack. "Is that not a paltry settlement to give me for my mother?"

"Well, then," said the gentleman, "I will give you twenty English pounds."

"Well," said Jack, "perhaps, since you are a gentleman, and doing as well as you are, perhaps you are not entirely to blame, and I may accept that and we will leave this matter as it is as long as you look after my mother and everything, and see that she gets a decent burial and is taken care of."

That was done, and Jack went back home. His bosses asked him if he had buried the old lady.

"I did not bury the old lady," he answered. "Why should I? I went and sold her."

"And how," said one of his bosses, "did you sell the old lady?"

"I went to town," said Jack, "and I called out to see if there was anyone who would buy an old lady. And they all gathered around and they began. One would say, 'I will give you so much for her,' and another would say, 'I will give you more than that for her,' and finally I got twenty pounds for her."

"And do you think," asked the other boss, "that we would get that for the other old lady?"

"I don't know what you could sell," replied Jack Fury, "but I believe that if I had had three old women, with the rush everyone was in to buy an old woman I could have sold all of them."

So the two bosses did away with the other old housekeeper that night and they took her to town to sell her. But the townspeople were so outraged that dogs were set on the two bosses and they had to flee, and hide in the woods.

Finally, the bosses reached home and they grabbed Jack and put him into a large sack, bound a string good and tight around the sack, and set out to drown him. But it seems that the day was quite warm and on their journey they threw the sack to the side of the road and continued on a short distance to where there was a tavern, to have a drink of beer before they went with Jack to cast him into the river. Soon Jack heard a sound down the road and he decided from the sound that it was a cattle-drover coming. When he heard the noise of the cattle walking by he began to complain and complain, saying, "I will not marry the king's daughter; I certainly will not. I will not marry the king's daughter in spite of them. Even if I were put to death I would not marry the king's daughter."

The drover came up to Jack. "What," said he, "are you saying?"

"I am saying," replied Jack, "that I will not marry the king's daughter. Why should I marry the king's daughter when I am in love with another maid? And now they are threatening to do away with me unless I marry the king's daughter."

"Well," said the drover, "I would marry the king's daughter."

"In that case," said Jack, "untie the string from the mouth of the sack and let me out. You can marry her. I don't want her at all." So the poor drover was put into the sack and the string was bound around it and Jack went off with the cattle.

When the others came out of the tavern the man in the sack was saying, "Oh yes, I'll marry the king's daughter."

"Do you hear," said one of the bosses, "what that soft-headed fool is saying?" They continued on with him and the man kept saying, "I will marry the king's daughter, I will marry the king's daughter."

Finally, the two bosses reached their destination and threw the drover into the river, and down he went with the current.

But a short time after they had returned home, there came Jack with a drove of cattle. He stopped up at the gate and hollered and hollered to the bosses until one of them finally said, "There's Jack back again. Go to meet him."

"I will not go to meet him at all," said the other. "I was afraid enough of him at the end of it when he was alive, and I will certainly not go near him now that he's dead."

The first one said, "Well, someone has to go to meet him, so we'll go down together."

They went out and Jack called to them, "Hurry up! Hurry up and open the gate and let in the cattle."

"And where," said one of the bosses, "did you get the cattle?"

"Didn't I find them," said Jack, "where you threw me? Down in the river. When I reached the bottom of the river, I never saw cattle so fine. There they were."

"Were they plentiful?"

"Plentiful!" said Jack. "If there were as many as four people with me, we could not have possibly caught all that were there. All I took was the worst of the drove. I did not have the time nor the help to take the rest."

"And do you think," said one of the bosses, "that if we were there, we would find cattle, too?"

"I don't know what you would find, but I know that if I had help, I could get many more cattle."

"Well," said the other boss, "you can take us to the place."

"I won't take you anywhere," said Jack. "Go there yourself."

"Oh," they said, "you have to take us there to see if we can get some more of those cattle."

"If you are so determined to go there," said he, "then I'll go with you. But you must go to the exact place where I went. It is not worth your while going anywhere else except for the place where I myself went."

And Jack took his bosses to a steep place with big rocks and a strong current. Jack had said to them, "Take along your own sacks. I'm not going to follow you with sacks at all," and when they arrived there one of the bosses was put in the sack and the sack was tied and Jack said to the other one, "You can throw him into the river." And as the man went under he made a gurgle of some sort.

"What did he say?" asked the other one.

"He said," Jack replied, "that he sees a large drove of cattle and they are just getting ready to flee from him."

"Quick," said the boss, "tie me in the sack."

"What sort of talk is that?" said Jack. "Won't you get in and be patient about it?"

"Oh, hurry, hurry!" he said. "I am in a hurry to go and help my friend." So Jack Fury put him into the sack and tied the string around it and rolled him down — and the second boss plopped into the stream.

And so it was that Jack Fury returned home with the big drove of cattle and the money he had gotten for the ox's hide and for the old woman — and all of these things he had for himself.

The Devil's Noodles

Dan Yashinsky

"I've always loved stories about beggars, tramps and street people who have unsuspected powers. Every Passover, our family set out the customary extra plate and glass of wine for Elijah. Jews believe that Elijah can appear as a road-rough wanderer, even a lowly beggar. But, if you show kindness to him, he will repay you with miraculous gifts. I've also always loved stories about people who can bedevil the Devil.

The Devil's Noodles is a mix of folk tales and real life. I really do know a man like Renato, and he really did run the best Italian café in Toronto. If the events in the story could have happened to anyone, they would probably have happened to him. What's a Jew doing, writing about Saint Peter? Well, he and and Elijah aren't all that different, and Saint Peter would be more likely to be walking through an Italian neighbourhood."

Once the Devil came to Toronto. He dropped by my friend Renato's café down in Little Italy, and ordered something that wasn't on the menu: Renato's soul. Poor Signor Diavolo, the dish didn't agree with him, and he's stayed away from

Toronto ever since. Here's the story, the way I heard it from Renato's wife Perry, who heard it from her husband, who says it's true.

Renato was the best cook in Little Italy. He was famous for his noodles, which he liked to serve with a spicy sauce full of hot peppers. He called this dish pasta alla diavola — hot-as-the-devil noodles. He even named the restaurant the Café dal Diavolo. I was always trying to get the recipe for his sauce, but Renato would never tell me the secret.

The noodles were spicy and so was the cook. He smoked too much, drank too much vino rosso, had a rough tongue, and spent too much money at the racetrack. The prices at the café rose and fell depending on how his horses ran that day. He never went to church, rarely paid his taxes, and sold illegal wine out of an unplugged freezer at the back. People used to say he was pazzo — crazy — and that he was a bit of a diavolo himsef. But for all his sins, he made everyone feel welcome: kids came by for biscotti after school, old men drank espresso and talked about soccer politics horses, people brought their bambini just so Renato could hug them.

Well, one day I was sitting at a table enjoying some pasta alla diavola and watching a parade outside on College Street. I think it was in honour of Saint Peter. The sidewalks were packed, a priest led a choir, a marching band played "I'll Do It My Way," a Cadillac full of soccer players drove by, everyone shouted *Viva Italia!* All of a sudden, the crowd pulled back. Right in front of the window where I was sitting an old man stumbled onto the sidewalk. His clothes were shabby, his beard was unkempt, his hair was sticking out every which way from under a broken-down old hat. And he was well and truly intoxicated.

Yes, this old man, he played nine, he'd been drinking too much wine! People looked at him and shook their heads in disgust. Imagine such a vagabondo — a tramp — spoiling a parade! When Renato saw the old tramp he hurried outside, wiped his hands on his apron, offered his arm, and brought him back into the café. He laid an immaculate white tablecloth, fetched a glass of "grape juice" from the freezer, and began to serve him a meal fit for a king. This old man obviously didn't have two pennies to rub together, but Renato fed him anyway — salad (he used to tell me that to make it right you had to crush the vegetables together with your hands, not toss them with salad forks), noodles, veal, a big cappuccino for dessert, all sprinkled with chocolate and cinnamon. I thought maybe Renato's horse had come in first that day.

The old man ate like he hadn't touched food for a week. He gobbled and guzzled and slurped and burped — it was not a pretty sight. By the time he was swallowing his coffee I'd had enough. I paid for my meal, thanked Renato, and left. If only I had stayed! The miracles we miss by leaving a minute too soon! Right after I left, the old tramp, who was the only customer at the time, ran away. Just what you might expect from a low-life type like that.

Renato had turned his back for a second and boom, the old guy was gone! But there in his place, drinking from the same coffee cup, was a new old man. This one was wearing a thousand-dollar white suit, a panama hat, beautifully shined Italian shoes — and he drank the vagabondo's cappuccino like a king sipping from a golden goblet. Renato's jaw hit the floor and his eyes hit the ceiling. "Who are you?" he cried. "Where'd that other guy go?"

The new old man rose from the table, made a courtly bow and said, "Allow me to explain. The tramp you served so generously — that was me."

"You!" Renato said. "What kind of magician are you, eh?"

"No magician," said the fine old gentleman, "but rather a saint. I go by many names, Renato, but your people know me as Saint Peter. I wander the earth dressed in the rags of a beggar, discovering who among you will be kind to a homeless tramp. Today I decided to visit Toronto. Alas, what a reception your fellow citizens gave me! You saw how they scorned me when I walked among them. You, on the other hand, have shown me true generosity. To reward you, I'm going to grant you three wishes. By the way, do you have a licence for that excellent wine you served me?"

"A licence?" said Renato, panicking. "Please sir, or saint, or magician, or whoever you are, I'm just a simple Italian cook trying to make a more or less honest living. Prego ... don't report me to the Inspector!"

"Ah, relax, Renato. I'm just teasing. I'm going to help you with your troubles, not add to them. What's your first wish?"

Renato thought for a moment, then said, "San Pietro, I'll tell you the truth. I already have everything I want or need. I've travelled the world, my wife loves me, I've got my café and my friends. What else do I need? The only other thing I've ever wanted was a bambino of my own, but if the Good Lord had wanted us to have kids, it would've happened before all these grey hairs showed up on my head. No, why don't you give my wishes to someone who could really use them."

"Can't," said Saint Peter. "Against the rules. They're yours or nobody's. How about gambling? You want me to fix it so you always win?"

"No," said Renato, "that would take all the fun out of it." Then he thought some more and started to grin. "Ha, Pietro, now I've got a good idea. You know how I like to play tricks sometimes. I like to fool around, have some fun. Well, you can help me play some real good — or maybe bad — tricks. You see these bar stools, the kind that go around and around? Well, most afternoons the boys come in after school and sit on them. They're not bad ragazzi, but sometimes I get mad when they don't get off and let the old men sit there. I want to teach them a little lesson. I wish that the next kid to sit on a bar stool gets stuck to it, and that it turns around and around, faster and faster, and the kid gets good and dizzy and really sick and …"

"Basta!" said Saint Peter. "Enough! You've just wasted a heavenly wish on a stupid practical joke. What's your second wish?"

"For my second wish," said Renato, "I'd like to teach another lesson. I used to be a blacksmith before I became a cook, and I made all my own pots and pans. See this cast iron pan? It's my favourite. Neighbours are always borrowing it, and I'm always telling them to treat it with respect. Dry it properly, put a bit of oil on for protection, otherwise it'll rust. But do they remember? No! Look, see here — a rust spot … My second wish is that I'd like to make anyone I want jump into the frying pan and cook their culetto. And," Renato hurried on — he could see the the saint was getting impatient, "my last wish is that if anyone suspicious comes into the café, like a tax collector or liquor inspector or, who knows, the Devil himself, I want them to hop into my freezer and stay there until I let them out."

"It's true what they say about you, Renato," said Saint Peter, "You really are a bit of a diavolo. Your wishes will come true, God help us. I have to go back to heaven now. By the way, try the fifth horse in the fifth race at five o'clock. Ciao!"

Renato waited until the fine-looking gentleman left. Then he took five hundred dollars and went to the racetrack. He bet it all on the fifth horse in the fifth race at five o'clock. Unfortunately, the horse came in fifth.

When Perry heard how much money he'd blown, she was furious. When he tried to explain that a saint from heaven had given him the tip, she threw a bowl of tortellini at him. Then she stomped out of the room and yelled, "May the Devil take you, you big idiot!"

Later that night, around midnight, just as Renato was sweeping up he heard a knock at the front door. When he opened it he was surprised to find a little boy standing there.

"What do you want?" he asked. "Isn't it past your bedtime?"

"My daddy sent me," said the boy. "He said you have to come with me, and he's a very big padrone, he's the biggest boss in the world, so you'd better come."

"Who's your daddy?"

The little boy grinned a wicked little grin, and Renato noticed he had two horns on his head. "My papa runs the Hot Place," said the boy devil, "and he says he's going to get you good."

Renato thought fast. Then he said, "Well, I'll be with you right away, I just have to finish cleaning up the place. Here, why don't you come in and have some biscotti — they're over by the counter."

The little devil walked over to the counter and jumped up onto a bar stool. No sooner did he sit down than the stool started spinning — faster and faster and faster until the little devil's face turned as green as a pickle in a blender.

"I'm … going … to be … very … sick …" he gasped as his head whipped around and around. "Help me!"

Renato left him on spin cycle for a minute or two, then he said, "Bar stool, stop! You get out of here, you little devil, and you go tell your big daddy that I'm not afraid of him or anyone else!"

"Yes sir, yes sir, yes sir!" panted the boy devil, as he wobbled to the door.

It all might have stopped there, but the very next day Renato woke up with a strong feeling that he should bet four hundred dollars on the fourth horse in the fourth race at four o'clock. He locked up early, took his money to the track, and placed his bet. The horse came in fourth.

This time Perry took the iron frying pan and chased him all over the café. "Fool!" she hollered. "That's money we need for our trip to Italy! May the Devil take you!"

Around midnight there was a knock at the door. When Renato opened it he found a teenager standing there. Half his head was shaved, the rest was bright purple. He was carrying a motorcycle helmet and he looked tough.

"Let's go," he said, without moving his lips much. "Papa hates waiting. He's real mad at you. My little brother's still cross-eyed."

Renato thought fast and said, "Look, before we go, I was just about to cook up some noodles alla diavola. How about a little midnight snack?"

"Uh," grunted the teenager, which means "yes" in Teenager. So Renato took the cast iron pan, poured in some extra virgin olive oil, turned on the heat, threw in some garlic, and waited for the oil to get smoking hot. Then he turned to the teenaged devil and said, "Hop aboard. We'll try cooking some diavolo alla diavola. I like my devils well done."

The teenager leapt up in the air and landed bum first in the burning oil.

He twisted and turned, but the pan kept toasting his buns. Renato chuckled. It was funny the way the big tough teenager kept bouncing around on his culetto.

"*Aieee!*" he cried. "*Lemme go!*"

"Say it nicely," said Renato.

"*Please!*" shouted the teenaged devil.

"Make up a poem. I'm in the mood for some poetry."

The devil's bottom was getting really scorched by now — he was desperate! He started rapping a poem:

"Mister Renato, please listen to me

Your frying pan causes me agony,

I beg you let me get out fast

Before it really burns my — "

"All right," laughed Renato, "get out, and don't ever come back."

The teenager jumped out of the frying pan and hobbled away as fast as he could.

Heaven, hell, horses, hot peppers — my old friend's head was just spinning. He went back to the racetrack the very next day and laid one thousand dollars on the first horse in the first race at one o'clock. It came in last.

When Perry found out she yelled, "Il gioco ha il diavolo nel cuore! Gambling has the devil in its heart! You've just wasted all of our savings, you ninny goony! May the Devil himself take you out of my life!" She stormed off, slamming every door in the place.

Renato sat on a bar stool and poured himself a glass of "grape juice." He was feeling pretty low. He'd never seen his wife so mad before. He'd never lost so much money before. Just then, there was a knock at the door. When he opened it he found a tall man wearing a black suit. Over by the curb was a limousine with smoked-glass windows. The tall man was wearing sunglasses.

"Renato," he said — his voice reminded Renato of the hiss hot iron makes going into cold water — "I've been looking forward to this meeting for a long time. We've got a nice welcome planned for you downstairs. Let's go, noodle-chopper. As they say, you can run but you can't hide."

"I never ran, and I'm not trying to hide," said Renato, more bravely than he really felt.

"Shut up and follow me," said the tall man.

"But Signor Diavolo, let's have a toast first. I've never met anyone as famous as you, and it would be nice to lift a glass of wine before you take me away. If you don't mind, I'll just finish writing my will while you go and get a bottle. It's in the freezer at the back."

The Devil wasn't averse to a glass of good Italian wine. He sauntered back and opened the freezer. Renato whirled around and shouted, "By all the powers of heaven, get in my freezer you big gangster!" The Devil jumped in, the lid crashed down, and Renato began to laugh. Then he walked over and plugged the freezer in. He turned the dial from *Normal* to *Coldest*. Then he made two cappuccinos, opened a box of Italian chocolates, and walked upstairs. Perry was watching TV. She turned it off when he came in.

"Mi amore," said Renato, offering her some chocolates and a cappuccino, "I won't gamble again. I'm sorry ..."

She kissed him. She sipped her coffee. Then she turned the lights off and pulled him closer. Then she turned the lights back on. "What's that strange sound?" she asked.

"Oh, I thought I'd see if the freezer still worked."

They turned the lights back off.

In the morning, Renato was down in the café just before sun-up. He saw the limo outside; it had a parking ticket. Then he walked over to the freezer and said, "Eh, popsicle, you still there?"

A few moans and cracking noises came from inside. Then he heard a voice hiss, "Pppleese ... lllett ... mmee ... gggo ..."

"Sure. But don't you ever come back to my neighbourhood again!"

He opened the lid and Signor Diavolo staggered out. He was blue, his teeth were chattering, his sunglasses were covered with frost. He walked stiffly to the door, and a trail of ice cubes fell out of his pants. He didn't look back.

Well, that's almost the end of the story. It wasn't long after these strange doings that Renato and Perry moved back to Italy. People said they were just one step ahead of the tax collector. Now there's a fruit store where the Café dal Diavolo used to be.

One day I got a letter from Perry. She wrote:

> *I have some good news and some bad news. The bad news is that our Renato is sick — bad liver and bad lungs, that's what the doctors say. The good news is he's sending you his recipe for the Devil's noodles: cook onions and garlic and tomatoes and pancetta and hot pepper; put in flakes of red pepper and some fresh ground black pepper; don't use that junk that's already ground up for you; cook some noodles and mix them with good olive oil and some parmesan cheese and a bit of romano cheese; grate your own and don't use that junk that's already grated for you; mix it up and eat it. There might be another ingredient, but he can't remember what it is. He says the medicine makes him kind of forgetful. Renato says not to worry about him. He figures Saint Peter probably won't let him into heaven — too much gambling, too little praying. But then he thinks the Devil's too scared to let him into hell. He says the Devil will probably give him a radicchio full of hellfire and tell him to go start a hell of his own somewhere. I don't know. I think our Renato would rather just open up another Café dal Diavolo somewhere on this sweet earth, and cook a lot more noodles for people to enjoy.*
>
> *Amore from both of us.*
>
> *Perry.*
>
> *P.S. How's the bambino?*

▼▼▼▼▼▼

The Raccoon Story

Lynda Howes

"The thing I like most to do is to listen to stories. That is
why I tell them."

▼▼▼

When our two daughters were still small enough to be called
children and yet big enough to pitch their own tent, my
husband and I took them camping.

We packed the family car and went down East to the
Gaspé, to Forillon National Park. There we found a campsite
on a rocky ledge amidst birch, balsam fir and spruce, over-
looking the Gulf of St. Lawrence.

By the time we set up camp, had our dinner and tidied
up, night had fallen. My daughters disappeared into their
tent and soon I could tell by the quiet that they were fast
asleep. I checked the embers to be sure the fire was out and
turned to go into our tent, when I noticed two marshmallows
lying on the picnic table. I took a cup that stood nearby and
turned it over the marshmallows. "My daughters can have
these in their hot chocolate in the morning," I thought. And
then I went to the tent.

I looked at the door. "How can I open this zipper without
making any noise?" I wondered. I began, slowly at first — zip,
zzip, zzzip — but this was taking far too long! I was tired and

anxious to get into my cozy sleeping bag. So I gave up trying to be quiet and opened the door — zip, zip, zip — with all speed. I crawled into the tent and closed the door — zip, zip, zip. Then I opened up my sleeping bag — zip, zip — climbed in and — zip, zip — I closed myself in.

At last, safe in the tent and snug in my sleeping bag, I waited to drift off into blissful slumber.

But that was not to be. I heard the crackling of branches and the rustle of leaves coming from the forest. And there were other noises — could there be a bird, or perhaps a four-footed beast, on the forest floor? I was still trying to identify the last strange sound when I heard something brush up against my tent. I looked over my shoulder. There was something there all right! I turned to my husband, but he was fast asleep.

Then I heard a sound coming from over by the table. I reached for my flashlight and shone it out the window of the tent and in the direction of the sound. There was a raccoon! It was up on the table and it was busy with the cup. I held the raccoon in the beam of light. At last, he stopped what he was doing, turned his head in my direction and I saw two dark eyes looking at me. Then the raccoon twitched his tail, climbed down from the table, made his way out of the campsite and disappeared.

"What a relief!" I thought as I nestled down in my sleeping bag. "Perhaps now I can get some sleep."

But I was wrong. Hardly had I said that, when I heard another sound from the table. This time it was louder. I reached for my flashlight and shone it through the window and onto the table. There was not just one raccoon. There were two raccoons and they were busy with the cup. I held the raccoons in the beam of light and they stopped and turned their heads. Now I saw four dark eyes looking at me. The raccoons twitched their tails, climbed down from the table, made their way out of the campsite and disappeared.

"Those raccoons are not going to get the marshmallows," I thought. Zip, zip — I climbed out of my sleeping bag. Zip, zip, zip — I opened the door of the tent, ran to the table, grabbed the marshmallows from under the cup, ran back into the tent — zip, zip, zip — closed the door, slipped back into my sleeping bag — zip, zip — and there I lay with the marshmallows, one in each hand.

Then I heard a chittery-chattery sound, a sound raccoons make when they are looking for something. I sat bolt upright, reached for the flashlight and shone it through the window. There were raccoons all right: not just one raccoon, not just two raccoons. There were five raccoons and they were all coming toward me. I held the raccoons in the beam of light and they stopped coming. They looked up and I saw ten dark eyes staring at me. They twitched their tails, turned out of the campsite and disappeared.

"What am I to do?" I wondered. "I want to go to sleep tonight, but I do not want those raccoons to get these marshmallows." And then I had an idea! "I'll put the marshmallows in my mouth and I'll swallow them."

I was about to pop the first marshmallow in my mouth when I hesitated. I thought: "All I want is to snuggle up in my sleeping bag and fall asleep, but what if a raccoon comes along? He could open the door, reach in, grope around till he finds my mouth and dig down into my stomach. Aaagh! He'll find the marshmallows."

"Oh no, you won't!" I shouted. Still my husband beside me remained fast asleep. I thought some more about raccoons — how they cannot get into places that have been locked with a key. "There is one place in our campsite we can lock with a key," I thought, "and that is the trunk of our car."

Zip, zip — I opened my sleeping bag. Zip, zip, zip — I opened the door of the tent. I ran over to the car and opened the trunk. I tossed in the marshmallows — one, two — closed the trunk and gave it a tug to make certain that it was locked, and then I ran back to the tent. I leaped inside — zip, zip, zip — closed the door, got into my sleeping bag — zip, zip — and there I lay.

I could hear the chittery-chattery sound. "Raccoons," I thought to myself, rolling over sleepily. As I lay there, the sound got noisier and noisier and noisier.

And then I heard a sound of a different sort. It went — *squeak, squeak, squeak.* "What is that?" I wondered. I reached for the flashlight and shone it at the car. There they were: the raccoons! They were on top of the car. There was not just one raccoon. There were not just two raccoons. There were not just five raccoons. There were twenty raccoons! There were raccoons on the hood of the car; there were raccoons on the roof of the car; and there were raccoons on the trunk of the car. And what do you know! The raccoons that were on the trunk were rocking the car up and down trying to get at the marshmallows.

I held the raccoons in the beam of light. At last they stopped rocking the car and looked in my direction. I saw forty dark eyes staring at me! The raccoons twitched their tails. They climbed down from the car, made their way out of the campsite and disappeared.

"Now what am I to do?" I wondered. "I want some sleep, but I will not let those raccoons get the marshmallows." And then a thought began to form itself in my head. I used to pitch for a girl's baseball team and have a reputation for possessing a strong arm. "I'll throw the marshmallows. I'll throw them far away. I'll throw them so far away the raccoons will never find them." All this I said through gritted teeth.

Zip, zip — I got out of my sleeping bag. Zip, zip, zip — I got out of the tent and ran to the car. I opened the trunk, reached in for the marshmallows, put one in each pocket and with the flashlight in my hand I made my way out of the campsite and through the shadowy forest toward the cliff's edge. I watched carefully where I put my feet. I did not want to trip on the underbrush. And all around me that chittery-chattery noise kept getting louder.

When I came to the top of the cliff, I reached inside my pockets and took out the marshmallows. Then I whipped around and held the marshmallows up, one in each hand. As I looked into the forest I saw eyes, hundreds of eyes. The raccoons were everywhere. They were peering out from behind trunks of trees, hanging from the branches and lurking behind boulders.

I turned towards the Gulf and prepared to throw. Keeping my eyes on a distant point across the water, I drew back my arm, aimed and threw one marshmallow. It flew out of my hand and up into the air and across the water in a great arc. I watched as it disappeared somewhere out there on the other side of the Gulf. "Good throw, Lynda!" I said to myself. I warmed up to throw the second marshmallow. As I watched it disappear, I sighed with satisfaction, "At last, the marshmallows are safe. The raccoons will never get them!"

I turned to make my way back to the campsite. Suddenly, something hairy and warm brushed up against my leg. I looked down. It was a raccoon! And then another raccoon brushed up against my other leg. I almost fell over the edge of the cliff! I looked over my shoulder. The raccoons were hustling to the top of the cliff; they were clambering down the steep bank; they were stepping into the water and they were swimming. I looked out at the water. It was crowded with raccoons. Why, the Gulf of St. Lawrence was solid raccoon for as far as I could see!

Later, safe in my tent, I slept.

In the morning, we broke camp and continued our holiday along the coast of New Brunswick. Ten days later we were returning to Toronto when my husband, the sound sleeper, suggested, "Let's camp at Forillon National Park again. It is so beautiful there!"

Before I would agree, I said I had to call the park warden and ask him a question.

"Warden," I said, "have you seen any raccoons recently?"

"It's strange you should ask," the warden replied. "Until recently, we had been having a lot of trouble with raccoons. They were getting into food coolers, tents and, on the odd occasion, into the trunks of cars. But as of about ten days ago, we haven't seen hide nor tail of a raccoon. They seem to have gone!"

As if anticipating my next question, the warden continued, "Where they've gone I can't be sure, but I got a call from a fishing guide on the island in the middle of the Gulf. He was shouting over the phone and talking so fast I could hardly make out what he was saying. As far as I could tell, he was saying something about raccoons — how they were climbing out of the water and up onto the island. He said, 'There have never been raccoons on this island before. Now there are hundreds!'"

The warden paused. It was dead quiet on the line. And then he added, "He said something that will puzzle me for the rest of my life. He said, 'Those raccoons seem to be looking for something!'"

P.S. I never played baseball as a kid. All the rest is true.

▼▼▼▼▼▼▼

Nanabush Stories
Gilbert Oskaboose

"The Creator, the Beginning, the Ojibway, Nanabush and the Legends: A Brief History and Explanation.

Long before the beginning times, before Creation, there was the Creator … and nothing more.

And the Creator had a vision.

In the vision, the Creator beheld countless stars, worlds beyond number, distance beyond measure, a Void beyond comprehension. He saw darkness and light, ice and fire, wind and water, and into them He breathed form and substance and meaning and purpose and Life. In the vision the Creator saw the sun and the moon and mighty rivers and rainbows and towering escarpments and endless lakes. He saw granite mountains and deep valleys and rain and snow and the changing seasons. In the vision the Creator saw oaks and maples and pine trees and wildflowers. He saw marsh grasses and blueberries and herbs and medicine plants. In the vision the Creator saw deer and moose and bears and wolves and beaver. He saw otter and mink and muskrats and lynx and rabbits and mice. In the vision the Creator heard the song of the wind and thunder and the eagle's scream. He heard the loon's cry and the music of waterfalls. In the vision the Creator tasted maple sugar and honey and strawberries. He tasted sweet water and wild rice and ripe corn and squash. In the vision He saw the Ojibway — First People.

In the vision the Creator sensed birth and growing and joy and love. He knew pain and sorrow and serenity. He felt contentment and awe and bitter disappointment and aging and dying. In the vision the Creator dreamed of different worlds and separate realities and great mysteries. He dreamed of strange and wondrous creatures — spirit helpers and demons and dreamspeakers and windwalkers — who would never know the limitations or the confines of flesh and blood and time and space.

Then the vision passed … and all of Creation flowed from the mind of the Creator into existence.

One of the many creatures that came from the mind of the Creator was a spirit woman. She lived alone out among stars and with the ones who wander the night sky. In her emptiness she asked the Creator for a companion. He heard her cries.

When her time came, she accepted the invitation of the four-legged, the swimmers, the winged and the crawlers of the Earth. She came down from the sky and gave birth to twins. They were a boy and a girl — the first Ojibway. Because she was of the spirit world and her two children were of the Earth, she had difficulty in raising them in the proper manner. And so the Creator sent the Wind to tell her and all the creatures how to raise the children.

The bear taught them to find shelter and honey. The wolf taught them to run and hunt. The beaver taught them how to swim and build strong lodges. The fox taught them cunning and the eagle gave them vision.

When her children had grown up, the spirit woman returned to the night sky. She lives there today, controlling the changing seasons, the tides and the time of women. The First People call her Grandmother. This is how we honour the First Mother.

The Ojibway flourished in the new world. Their numbers grew until a terrible sickness came and they became like dead leaves before the winds of winter. Great sorrow and pain came to the People. The Creator heard their cries and sent four spirits to teach them wisdom, medicine and the Way of the Sacred Pipe and Drum.

Born of the west wind and a human mother, the four spirits each gave many teachings. They did wondrous deeds and left many legacies to the Ojibway.

Greatest of the teachers was Nanabush — the Trickster. Nanabush's gift to the Ojibway is the nature of wisdom and knowledge. He teaches, by his words and actions, through humour, through terrible mistakes and in great accomplishments what the Ojibway should do and what they should not do. Nanabush is godlike, noble, and wise — and he is foolish, boastful and cruel. Nanabush is old and young, beautiful and ugly, smart and stupid, generous and greedy, kind and hateful. He is the apex of all that is good in the Ojibway and he is the zenith of all that is bad in us! Nanabush is all we can be and all we limit ourselves to being.

Nanabush is still here, in the mischievousness and cruelty of children. He is here in the pride of youth and in the vanity of physical beauty. We can sense him in the wisdom of the Elders. We can hear his laughter in the folly of those who have travelled the Sacred Hoop of Life — and are none the wiser for the trip. The Ojibway honour Nanabush and carry on his teachings in the legends."

▼▼▼

Nanabush and the Black Duck

A long time ago, when the world was young, the most beautiful bird in all the forest was Black Duck.

His brilliant plumage seemed to have caught and held the rainbows: iridescent greens, shimmering indigo, scarlet reds, sky blues and blinding whites. He had them all!

He was forever admiring his reflection in pools or bragging to the other creatures about how handsome he was. Sometimes creatures that are too "good looking" are like that.

When Nanabush heard this he decided to teach Black Duck a good lesson. So Nanabush let it be known that he was throwing a big party to honour his friend Black Duck.

"And rightfully so," thought Black Duck, preening himself in the reflection of a small puddle. "This will be an excellent opportunity to show the rest of the drab folk who is the most handsome in all the forest."

At the party, all the food, the glory and the homebrew were just too much, and Black Duck passed out cold.

Nanabush instructed the other birds to line up and exchange all of their dull drab feathers for the colorful ones of Black Duck. And so that's what they did.

Woodpecker took the brilliant red ones from the top of Black Duck's head; Bluebird and Jay took all of the sky blue ones; Finch and Grosbeak divided all of the yellow ones and Seagull ended up with all the white ones ... and so on ... As the birds took all of Black Duck's beautiful feathers they left their own drab ones in exchange, because Nanabush had taken pity on Black Duck and didn't want him to go naked.

When Black Duck woke up and realized what had happened to him he felt a great shame, and fled deep into the forest to hide from everyone.

And that is where Black Duck lives to this very day, alone and secretive and rarely seen by anyone. That is how the birds got their colours and how Black Duck got his.

And that's the end of the story.

Nanabush and the Turkey Vulture

Long ago and far away — when the world was young — Nanabush was out for a stroll on the beach one day when he spotted Vulture circling far overhead.

In those times Vulture was a handsome fellow and he knew it! His head was covered with fine feathers that had every colour of the rainbow. He was forever admiring his reflection in the ponds and never wearied of asking the other birds "who was the most handsome," although they certainly grew tired of him asking the same question.

Now Nanabush knew all this and so he said to himself: "Waugh! There's Vulture way up there. Probably looking for an eagle to brag to. I've got a good mind to teach that bugger a lesson!"

Nanabush was like that, you know, always straightening people out and teaching lessons to whoever had it coming.

And so that's was Nanabush did. He laid down on the beach and magically turned himself into a dead bear. He lay very still and watched out through his eyelashes.

He didn't have to wait too long before Vulture spotted him. Aside from being too handsome, Vulture also was very sharp-sighted.

Down Vulture came, slowly, in ever diminishing circles. He was in no hurry; his dinner wasn't going anywhere, and who knows, he might just happen to meet Seagull along the way.

Nanabush lay very still.

When Vulture finally landed, he stood off at a safe distance and threw a good sized rock at the bear, just to make sure it was really dead and not just "playing possum."

The rock bounced off the bear's head and made Nanabush's eyes water but he didn't move a muscle or cry out. He knew this was an old hunting safety trick he had taught the Ojibway so they wouldn't get hurt by wounded animals.

Vulture was convinced everything was okay so he hopped up to the dead bear and started pecking away. He pecked and pecked until his pecker got sore; the bear's hide was just too tough for him to get through.

"There must be an easier way," Vulture said, walking around the bear, deeply puzzled.

"Aha, there it is," he said, spotting the wide open anus Nanabush had arranged for him to see. He stuck his head in and started looking around for tender pieces like liver and kidney.

That's when Nanabush sprung his trap. His backside snapped shut and Vulture was caught.

He flapped his wings, he scratched and kicked, and he even yelled as best he could, but to no avail. He was caught, and the harder he struggled the harder Nanabush hung on, which was very difficult to do — hang on tight and laugh at the same time.

After about an hour or so Nanabush took pity on him, as Nanabush is wont to do at times, and let him go. Vulture staggered down to the water to wash his head and was horrified when he saw his reflection.

The fine coloured feathers on his head were all gone. All that was left was a red wrinkled head and neck that looked like they had been soaking in dishwater too long. Vulture was deeply ashamed and flew away to be by himself. And that's why, to this very day, Vulture is secretive, shy, very cautious, and looks the way he does.

And that's the end of the story.

Nanabush and the Dogs

Once upon a time, long ago and far away, as these matters usually are, all the dogs came together for a big meeting. In those days dogs could speak, just like humans, so this big meeting was not as strange as it sounds, at least not for that reason.

All the dogs were there: big ones, small ones, fat ones, skinny ones, young ones, old ones, handsome ones, ugly ones and so on and so on. They were all there.

In those times it was the custom to hang one's tail on a nail just inside the door, much the same way we hang up our hats today when we enter a lodge, out of respect.

With the dogs it was easy because the anus attached to the tail made a dandy ring to slip over a nail. Some of the dogs even became quite skillful at tossing the ring over the nail from ten or fifteen feet away. They say that is how the modern game of "ring-tossing" was invented, but that's another story, for another time.

Once the meeting got going everybody started yapping at once, except of course, the ones that always come to meetings and never say anything. They save their words for later, for the "moccasin telegraph" or for when they're drunk, and not afraid of anyone.

In the meantime, at the meeting, everybody else was mixing it up. Big dogs growled, little dogs yapped shrilly, old dogs criticized everything, silly dogs clowned and vicious dogs attacked anything that moved. Whenever a dog fell down, or was knocked down, the rest would pounce on it and give it a damn good beating. To add to the confusion all the crazy dogs howled for no apparent reason.

Nanabush happened to be going by at the time and heard all the commotion. The racket hurt his ears and he became very annoyed at the dogs' behaviour.

"I've got a good notion to play a trick on those noisy buggers," he said, digging around for his fire-starter. In no time at all Nanabush had the back wall of the council lodge burning fiercely. Then he ran away laughing.

Inside, the dogs smelled the smoke, saw the flames and panicked.

Everybody headed for the door at the same time; it was every dog for itself.

In the confusion and panic no one took the time to find his or her own tail; they just grabbed one, stuck it on and ran for their lives.

And that is why, to this very day, whenever two strange dogs meet the very first thing they do is check out each other's backside and tails.

They're still trying to find their own.

And that's the end of the story.

▼▼▼▼▼▼

How Trickster Brought Fire to the People

Lenore Keeshig-Tobias

"Trickster stories are traditional stories, also called teachings. Trickster is central to these teachings and is probably the most loved character of all Native stories. It is through Trickster's transgressions and sins, as well as virtues, that we learn. More often than not, we learn not to do as Trickster has done.

'Blackflies and mosquitoes like these stories.' That is what Gladys Kidd, an Ojibway elder, advised me. This is the reason traditional stories are told only when the snow stays on the ground. In other words, she was telling me these stories are for certain ears only — Native or non-Native. If you want to share this story with others, please do so only in winter.

This story reminds me of another one of Gladys Kidd's teachings. She says, 'Animals can live without people, but people cannot live without animals.' I am also reminded that 'If all the animals of the world were to disappear, man would die of a great loneliness of heart.' These are the words of Chief Seattle of the Dwamish Nation."

A long time ago people had no fire. They huddled together in their lodges to keep warm during the cold seasons. And that was all right, because that was the way things were. But there came a time when the cold persisted, stretching out into too many dark cold days. Snow fell thick and heavy over the land. It became so cold that the thickness of fur robes and blankets could not keep the chill away. Even the closeness of their family and friends was not enough to keep the people warm. The cold was biting. And the people began to worry. They worried about their old people, their elders. They worried about their young people, the future.

And soon the people began to cry out in fear and misery.

It so happened that Trickster was going along about that time. (Back then, Trickster was always travelling somewhere.) He heard the people crying out and they cried out to him. "Older Brother, it is so cold. Please help us. We are worried about our young people and our old people. The cold will kill us all." Trickster asked the people to call council. They did. Trickster and the people talked and talked. Trickster agreed to go in search of fire and bring it back to the people.

The people gave Trickster food and moccasins for the long journey. And Trickster set out. He travelled for many days and many nights, and many days and many nights, until at long last he came to the foot of a great mountain. Then he climbed for many days and many nights, and many days and many nights, until he found himself walking around on the mountaintop.

After walking around for a bit, Trickster soon came to realize that he didn't really know what he was looking for.

Council had talked about fire, said that fire had bright coloured tongues and that these coloured tongues gave warmth like the sun. The only tongues Trickster knew were people tongues and animal tongues, and these were usually pink. Trickster looked for a ball. The sun, after all, was ball-like. And then he found himself looking for a ball with tongues on it, and then a tongue with balls on it. You see, he really didn't know what he was looking for except that it was something called "fire."

Finally, Trickster decided to ask his Huckleberry sisters what to do. They were very wise and would help him. So, he found himself a nice quiet place, squatted down and pooped.

Huckleberries are fragile little creatures. They bruise easily. And these Huckleberry sisters always travelled with their brother. The safest way for the sisters to travel was for Trickster to carry them in his stomach.

"Sisters, sisters," said Trickster, looking down at his sisters, "I need your help. I have to get fire for the people."

The sisters talked amongst themselves first and then told Trickster, "Listen, brother, we are not so sure if we can help you."

Trickster blinked in amazement. "Why not?" he asked.

"Brother," the sisters went on. "Every time we give you advice, tell you how to do things, you always say you knew how to do it all along."

"That's not true," said Trickster.

"Is too," answered the sisters.

"Is not," responded Trickster.

"Is too," said the sisters.

Trickster could have stood there all day arguing with his sisters. In fact, he could have stood there all week or longer arguing. You know how some sisters and brothers are. But Trickster was desperate this time. The people were counting on him. And he really didn't need to stand around and argue with anyone.

Trickster remembered that his sisters were afraid of hail. He planted his feet firmly apart, raised his arms into the sky and called out, "Hail, hail come down from the sky. Hail, hail come down from the sky. Hail, hail …" Great dark clouds began to roll in over the mountaintop.

The Huckleberry sisters trembled and cried out, "Oh Brother, don't call the hail. Don't call the hail. Please. We'll tell you what you want to know."

Trickster called out to the sky once more. "Hail, hail," he called. "Go away." The great dark clouds rolled quietly away. Trickster sat down beside his Huckleberry sisters.

"All right, Brother, listen carefully. This is what you must do. The first thing you have to do is go back down the mountain and have council with the animals … when the council is over you must come back up the mountain. Scout around in that direction and you will find a camp. At the centre of that camp you will see those coloured tongues you are looking for. You will also see three old fire-keepers. They will not give fire to you or anyone else. They don't want people to have fire. They don't want people to become as powerful as they themselves are. But, Brother, find yourself a good hiding spot and wait. Don't fall asleep. Those fire-keepers will take turns guarding and feeding the fire. When the night begins to settle over the mountain, two of those old fire-keepers will go into the lodge. That will leave one old fire-keeper to guard the fire for the night. Watch her. She will pick up a stick of wood and feed it to the fire. The fire will lick it and begin to eat. This will go on all night. Don't fall asleep now because when the ribbon of daylight appears on the horizon, that old fire-keeper will get up, go over to the lodge, scratch on the lodge pole, and say, 'Sister, sister. Get up and guard the fire.' That, Brother Trickster, is when you rush in and take for yourself a brand of fire. And then you must run. Run like you have never before run."

Trickster stood up, feet firmly apart. He placed his hands on his hips, nodded his head and stared off into the distance as if in great thought. "That's what I was thinking all along," he said.

Trickster made his way down the mountainside. It took him many days and many nights to get up the mountainside, so it took him just as many days and nights to get down the mountainside. He called a council of all the animals. That took a bit of time. Some of the animals had to travel a great distance to get there. Many words went around that council and when it was over, Trickster made his way back up the mountainside.

He found the camp of the fire-keepers and a neat little hiding place for himself. All day long he watched the fire-keepers tend to their business around the fire. He saw how they fed the fire with sticks of wood. He saw the coloured tongues lick the wood. Nighttime began to settle over the mountain and Trickster settled down for the long night ahead.

Just as his sisters had said, two of the old fire-keepers retired to the lodge. The other fire-keeper took up watch beside the fire. She picked up a stick of wood and fed it to the fire. The coloured tongues licked it hungrily, danced up into the night air, and as the wood slowly disappeared they danced down close to the ground. The fire-keeper then gave another stick of wood to the hungry flames. The red, the yellow and the orange tongues, dancing all the while, licked the wood and sent sparks jumping up into the darkness.

Trickster watched as the fire-keeper fed the dancing tongues stick of wood after stick of wood after stick of wood. Such colours — such dancing — he'd never seen before. It was beautiful. It was mesmerizing.

The fire-keeper picked up another stick of wood, put that into the flames. The coloured tongues licked it, savouring its flavour, sending sparks off into the darkness again and again. By this time Trickster was getting sleepy. His eyelids began to slip down over his eyes. His head nodded heavily. He was just about to let his eyes close in sleep when he saw it. Through his eyelashes, he could see the line, the ribbon of daylight. He shook himself awake and sat up. It wouldn't be long now.

The old fire-keeper rose slowly. She made her way over to the lodge where her sisters slept. She scratched on the lodge pole and said, "Sisters, sisters. Get up and guard the fire." It was the moment Trickster had been waiting for. He crept quickly into the centre of the camp, and scooped up a burning brand of fire, and ran away as fast as he could. Churning up snow and ice behind them, the three old fire-keepers chased Trickster down the mountainside. They were old, but how they ran! They were so close that Trickster could feel their hot breath on his neck.

Trickster jumped over crevices, ran around boulders and rolled like a snowball partway down the mountain. On and on he ran, faster than he had ever run in his life. On and on. He made his way down to the tree line, and there he fell — *splat!* on his face. He couldn't run anymore.

Cougar was there. Cougar was there hiding in the trees, waiting for him. She snatched up the brand of fire and raced away, heading for the high trees, the tall trees further down the mountain. Over the boulders, around the boulders, and through the trees she raced, on and on. The fire-keepers were right behind her too. Cougar could feel their breath hot on her neck. She raced as far as she could with the brand of fire, right up to the tall trees. There she handed the brand of fire over to Fox.

Now Fox ran, skilfully weaving his way through the tall trees, his tail sailing out behind as he ran. Fox headed straight for the heavy undergrowth. There Squirrel waited. Squirrel took the brand of fire from Fox and shot up to the treetops, and leapt from branch to branch to branch. The fire-keepers could not go through the heavy undergrowth, nor could they travel through the treetops, and so they planned to catch Squirrel at the edge of the meadow when she came down from above.

But the fastest of all the animals, Antelope, was there, waiting. He took the brand of fire from Squirrel and bounded across the meadow and over the other fields.

That is how it was. Each animal took a turn running for the people, carrying fire for the people, all the while chased by the old fire-keepers.

Finally there was only a glowing coal left, and this was passed on to Frog. Frog swallowed it and hopped away. The fire-keepers were right over top of Frog, ready to scoop her up. The little green hopping creature would be easy to catch, but Frog leapt into the river. She let herself sink down into its cool depth and then propelled herself in long steady strides toward the other side. Meanwhile the fire-keepers hurried back and forth along the river bank looking for a place to cross. The youngest of the three old creatures reached the other side first and was waiting for Frog, ready to pounce on her when she reached the river bank. Frog saw what was happening and immediately hopped between the legs of the old creature and hurried away. It wasn't long before all three creatures were behind Frog ready to catch her here as she jumped, there as she jumped. Frog continued on — hop, hop, hop. Finally, too tired to go on, she coughed up the hot coal. It landed on Wood and disappeared.

The fire-keepers could not figure out what had happened to the fire. Where did it go? How did it disappear so quickly? Did someone else take it? Then who? But even the animals were asking the same questions. Finally the old fire-keepers decided to go back and tend the fire they already had on the mountain.

None of the other animals knew what had happened to the fire. Poor Frog. She felt bad. She had tried her best and now there was no fire. It had disappeared. The other animals began to wonder too. They wondered if they had to do it all over again, run for the people. They wondered if they *could* do it again.

Trickster, the one to begin the relay, took his time catching up to the others. Along the way, he gathered bits of dry moss, some dry grass and twigs. He also searched for and found himself a nice thin length of hardwood. The animals gathered round as Trickster entered their midst. He put down his small bundle of moss, grass and twigs, and carefully pulled from his pouch the hardwood stick.

He placed one end of the stick on Wood and pressed the rest of the stick between the palms of his hands. He rubbed his hands together and twirled the stick. The harder he rubbed the faster the stick twirled. Everyone wondered what on earth was happening. Trickster twirled the stick again and again, and soon a thin ribbon of smoke curled up out of Wood. Trickster continued twirling the stick and more smokey ribbons danced up out of Wood. Then the sparks jumped out of Wood and disappeared in the air. Trickster moved the dry moss and grass closer to Wood, and twirled the stick again. Sparks jumped out onto the moss and grass, smouldered and then burst into small coloured tongues. Trickster fed the dry twigs to the coloured tongues. The coloured tongues grew and danced before the people.

After that people knew how to make fire. They learned how to cook their food. They kept their lodges warm and were seldom cold again.

As for Trickster, he kept on travelling. When he entered Ojibway territory, the people called him Nanabush or Nanabojoh. The Cree called him Wesakejak. Out on the prairies he was known as Coyote or Old Man Coyote. Up north he was called Hare. In the east he was Glooscap. He didn't care what people called him. He just kept on travelling. He had work to do.

Lovers

Voiceover

Ah, love. A storyteller I know once said that there are two kinds of love: "love" and "LLLUHVVVVV!!!" The stories in this section show you men and women loving and, if I can coin a term, misloving each other. From the stubborn spouses who argue about who'll tie up the cow, to the hapless princess who must decide how to use her third wish, the stories in this section show that intimacy is no easy matter between human beings. It is hard to earn someone's trust, hard to earn and keep their respect, hard not to judge them for their so-obvious faults (one's own never seem to be quite so bad), hard to keep talking when you want to rush off in a huff.

One of the stories, *The Wall of Glass*, was written by a high-school English student from a dream she had. In her dreamworld you can recognize all the hopes and disappointments that come with love. In the story about the Chinese heroine Lady Meng, tragedy ensues when lovers are separated by the capricious power of an emperor. You will also find in this section a grand epic from the Ojibway storyteller Esther Jacko. It is a mix of the romantic and the horrific. I heard Esther tell about Nungoose, Nimki and the terrifying Lupi the Great White Wolf late one February night, when the land was covered with snow and ice. You can imagine how I slept that night …

117

Va Attacher la Vache!

Justin Lewis
(from a folktale
told by Camille Chiasson)

"The last time I was in my home town, Sudbury, I went
downtown to the dignified old mansion which is the
home of the Centre Franco-Ontarien de Folklore. I
wanted to visit Père Germain Lemieux, whose
collections of folktales — one product of the careful
listening to old storytellers he has been doing since
1948 — have given me nearly all the French-Canadian
stories I tell. Père Lemieux is a small, white-haired,
happy man. When I arrived, he was working on a carved
wooden relief of La Chasse-Galerie, the 'witch canoe'
the lumberjacks told about. He interrupted his work to
show me his sketch of the scene: the lumberjacks in
their canoe, looking up fearfully at a great, leering devil
about to lift them into the skies.

Then he showed me around the Centre, a museum
and resource library for Franco-Ontarian culture. On the
walls are other carvings of his: a picture of an old church
in the neighbourhood, a scene from a Ti-Jean story. I got
to hear opera played on a wind-up gramophone and, at
my request, watch a video of one of his old storytellers.

In a large room upstairs, we said hello to the local artists and students who are producing the first volume of Ti-Jean comics. Unfortunately there are no videos of Monsieur Camille Chiasson (1880-1963), of Baie Sainte-Anne (New Brunswick) and Sudbury.

Père Lemieux remembers him as an old sailor, a giant of a man with a face tanned and sculptured by the ocean winds, a man who enjoyed remembering and talking, with a rich Acadian accent and a sonorous bass voice.

This story is based on an episode in a story told by Camille Chiasson, one of many he heard as a young man working winters in the lumber camps, and retold in his seventies on his lunch breaks from his full-time caretaking job at Collège Sacré-Coeur in Sudbury. He called the story 'Les Trois Fous de Russie,' and Père Lemieux has published it as the first story in Volume 21 of *Les Vieux M'Ont Conté*, his great collection of folktales."

▼▼▼

La semaine passée, la — last week, I was sitting at home, down on the farm. I was reading the paper, my wife was doing the dishes after supper, and la vache — the cow — was tied up by the side of the house, eating grass.

A few minutes later, moi, je lis le journal, my wife is doing the dishes, and la vache — is tied up by the side of the house, eating grass.

Ten minutes after that, moi, je lis le journal. My wife is doing the dishes. But la vache is tied up by the side of the house, eating grass.

Just then — moi, je lis le journal. My wife is doing the dishes. And — you'll never believe this — la vache — is tied up by the side of the house, eating grass.

Life's awfully quiet down on the farm.

But all of a sudden — the wind blew in through the window, grabbed mon journal, my newspaper, out of my hand, and threw it right out the other window, into the cow's face.

La vache was so scared she broke her rope, ran out into the field and started to eat our cabbages.

Well, you can't let things like that happen down on the farm. I got up. I went outside. I gathered up mon journal. I came back in. I sat down. Et je lis le journal.

My wife said, "Justin, go tie up the cow — va attacher la vache."

And I said, "Darling, va attacher la vache — go tie up the cow."

And she said, "Justin, can't you see I'm working? Va attacher la vache!"

And I said, "Sweetheart, can't you see I'm resting? Va attacher la vache!"

"Va attacher la vache!"

"Va attacher la vache!"

We argued like that for two hours and thirty-five minutes. Finally my wife said, "Okay, Justin. If that's the way you're going to be, the next one who talks — va attacher la vache."

"…"

"…"

Fine! I didn't say anything, she didn't say anything — the first one to talk would go tie up la vache. When my wife was finished the dishes, she went up to the attic, where I wouldn't see her and she wouldn't see me. She wouldn't even think of talking to me. Moi, I sit there, et je lis le journal.

Someone knocked at the door.

I went to let them in. It was my wife's brother. He said, "Bonjour, Justin! Haven't seen you for months! How have you been? Comment ça va?"

"…"

He said, "Justin, how are you? What's new? Hi!"

"…" (I'm not saying anything. I don't want to tie up that cow — je veux pas attacher la vache!)

"Um, Justin, is your wife here, my sister? Is she home?"

"…"

"Justin, where is she? Where's my sister?"

"…"

He started looking around. He looked in the kitchen. He looked in the bedroom. He looked in the bathroom. He didn't think of looking in the attic. He got worried.

"Justin, where is she?"

"…" (I'm not saying anything. Je veux pas attacher la vache!)

"Justin, where did you put her? What have you done to your wife?"

"…"

"Justin — did you kill your wife?"

"…"

He said, "Justin, je vais téléphoner la police!"

"…"

And he did. And two big police officers burst into my house. They grabbed me by the collar. They lifted me off the floor. They said, "Justin, where's your wife? Did you kill her? Where is she?"

Well, they dragged me out of the house and dragged me into court. The lawyers were there, the judge, all asking me questions: "Where is your wife? Why did you kill her? Where did you hide the body? How did you kill her? Did you kill your wife, yes or no?"

"…"

The judge said, "Justin, this is serious. If you don't say anything, I'll find you guilty. And if I find you guilty, we'll hang you! You understand? Speak or die. Did you kill your wife — *oui* or *non*?"

"…" (I don't want to die. But … je veux pas attacher la vache.)

"Coupable! Guilty! Take him out and hang him!"

And they dragged me outside and took me up onto the gallows and put the noose around my neck.

News travels fast in the country. In about two minutes a crowd gathered to watch me hang. All my friends were there, crying. All my enemies were there, laughing. And my wife was there, way in the back of the crowd! I wanted to say hi to her, but — je veux pas attacher la vache.

And they began to count down ten seconds to my death: "Dix."

"…"

"Neuf."

"…"

"Huit. Sept. Six. Cinq. Quatre … "

Oh, mon Dieu — in three seconds I would be dead. I thought, maybe I should say something? Tell them I didn't do it? Point to my wife, show them she's alive? Save my life?

And then I thought — Non! Je veux pas attacher la vache! "Trois."

"…"

"Deux."

"…"

"UN …"

It was the last moment of my life. I closed my eyes. I thought of my dear wife, how much I loved her. I thought — Je vais pas attacher la vache!

And suddenly, before they could spring the trap door, I heard a voice shouting out: "Don't hang him! Don't hang him!" It was my wife's voice — shouting from the back of the crowd — "I'm alive! Idiot! Espèce de fou! Don't hang him!"

Aah!

My life was saved. I opened my eyes, I took the noose from around my neck. Everyone was staring at my wife. I ran down from the gallows. I ran to my dear wife who saved me, I looked in her eyes and said: "Darling — you talked first! Va attacher la vache!!"

The Wall of Glass

Deanne Mallard

"*The Wall of Glass* is a vivid dream that I once had. I
wrote it down immediately and then it got pushed back
into a drawer in my desk. I forgot about it for several
months and struggled with another piece I was trying to
write. At this point my mind kept turning back to my
dream, and so I dug it out of my desk drawer and began
working on it. As I became more familiar with my story
it became clear that it was a story meant for telling. A
friend helped me to analyze parts of the dream but, as
yet, I don't fully understand its meaning. For that I am
grateful, because my story still holds some mystery for
me."

I dreamt of a young man. He was following a path he had
never taken before. It led into a deep forest where the trees
grew very tall and were lush and green. On either side of the
path ferns and grasses grew, covering the forest floor. The
path itself was overgrown and little-travelled.

The young man walked along the shady, winding path for
some time; then he suddenly felt the warmth of the sun.
There, in a clearing, was a large manicured lawn with a stone

path leading to an elegant white mansion. Two fluted pillars stood on either side of the front wall. This wall was made of glass, and through the panes he could see a room, its walls decorated with rich tapestries. Behind the wall of glass the young man could see a young woman. She was sitting in the only chair in the room. She was very still and stared vacantly out the window.

As soon as the young man laid eyes on the woman, he fell in love. Even though she was not overly beautiful, he was filled with wonder and amazement at her. He was so moved, he sat for hours at the edge of the lawn and admired her.

The next day he returned, and every day after that. In my dream he always did the same thing. He sat on the edge of the lawn and admired the young woman. Then, one day, he decided that he could no longer simply sit and watch her. He vowed that he would return the next day and ask her to marry him.

The next morning the young man once again set out on the path. He had been walking for some time when suddenly an old, old man appeared in front of him. In my dream this old man was thin and bony; he had hardly any hair. His eyes were deep set and his cheeks hollow. He looked sternly at the young man and said, "There is a deed that must be done if you want your marriage to survive. It can be done either now or shortly after the marriage. But it must be done. Do you accept the deed?"

"Yes, yes," the young man answered, and quickly continued on his way.

He had almost reached the estate when an old, old woman appeared on the path before him. She had long white hair and beautiful, wise eyes and yet in my dream she appeared somehow youthful. Smiling kindly at the young man, she said "There is a deed that must be done if you want your marriage to survive. It can be done now or shortly after the marriage. Do you accept the deed?"

Again the young man, eager to be on his way, agreed. He continued down the path and when he reached the mansion, he proposed to the young woman. She accepted and they were married. So, happy with one another and very much in love, the young couple lived together in the mansion. Soon after, they had their first child.

I dreamt the young man walked again in the forest. He found a little clearing nearby and in it, a beautiful garden. A stone path wound throughout the garden, which was filled with flowers of different colours and scents, and bushes and other such things. Every day he would walk there because the garden gave him great joy and peace.

One day, as he walked in the garden, he met the old man, who asked him, "Have you done the deed yet?" and the young man, filled with shame, answered "No." The old man became very sad when he heard this, but he said nothing and only watched as the young man continued on his way.

The next day, when the young man walked in the garden he met the old woman. She asked him "Have you done the deed yet?" and once again the young man admitted that he had not. In my dream, the old woman shook her head as she watched the young man slowly walk away.

Every day after that, the young man met the old man and woman in the garden, and every day they asked him the same question. He could not stand to see them so sad, yet he felt his marriage was as strong as it could be. What was the sense in doing some mysterious deed when he and his wife were so happy? The young man stopped walking in the garden. By this time, he and his wife had their second child. But the young man, although happy at the birth of his child, could not help but notice a loss. He had lost the peace he had enjoyed in the garden. He had begun to notice that his wife, too, was changing. She had become silent and was no longer happy.

One beautiful sunny day, the young man entered the room with the wall of glass. There was no curtain drawn across the window yet the room was dark and shadowy. He saw that his wife lay naked on a divan. Nearby were his children; the youngest was crying pitifully. Rushing over to the child, he comforted him, but the child would not stop crying. He tried to feed his child but did not know how. He looked to his wife for help but she did not acknowledge his presence and only stared vacantly, just as she had done when the young man had first seen her.

At that moment, the young man realized he had to find the old man and old woman. He had not seen them for many days and could only hope that it was not too late to do the deed and make things right again. He gently laid down the child and took one last look at his wife. Then I dreamt that the desperate young man ran from the mansion and out, out into the garden.

The Third Wish

Ricky Zurif

"I think of myself as a modern, urban storyteller, taking the raw material of my life and molding and shaping and editing it into witty, yet poignant, tales. Or to put it another way, I make it all seem very funny and loopy and meaningful, whereas, in reality, it was one long pointless disaster. So I'm not really at ease with fairy tales or folk tales or myths or any genres that are not about something that could have happened an hour ago in Montreal.

This story represents a departure for me. One of my students, Susan Chang, wrote a traditional fairy tale and I updated it with modern sensibility. It was transcribed from a live performance. I never write my stories down. For me the story is not alive until I get up on stage and deliver it personally."

Once upon a time, in a beautiful and peaceful kingdom, there lived a King and a Queen who were good, and who were decent, and who ruled the kingdom well. They had everything they wanted, but for one thing — and that was a child. And then, one day a child was born to them. They raised all the flags on the balconies of the castle, and they sent out the messengers to announce the good news, and they tolled all the bells of the kingdom, and they prepared a grand party.

Now, the child that was born to them was a little girl. She was extraordinary. She was very delicate, and very beautiful. She had lovely blonde curls and large blue eyes with long lashes, and a little turned-up nose, and full lips, and rosy cheeks; and everything about her was perfect. So that when it came time at the party for all the magic fairies of the kingdom to bestow a gift, they were hard-pressed to know what to give her. They looked at her and their hearts sank a bit; because, while they had planned to give her exquisite hair, she had that; and while they had planned to give her delicate, dewy skin, she seemed to have that too. So during the entire dinner they thought about what they could give her.

And then when the time came for the gift giving, one fairy said, "I give her the most beautiful singing voice imaginable!" And another one said, "I give her the ability to walk with such grace and such poise that people will turn and stare." And another said, "I give her compassion beyond all human imagination." And so on, until she had not only every beauty and grace, but all the finest virtues that one would wish for in a human being.

And then it came time for the last fairy. She approached the tiny Princess with rage in her heart. Don't ask me why. She had been seated at the head table with the rest of the fairies, she had eaten off gold plates, she had sipped the excellent champagne from the royal cellars. So it's not that she'd been snubbed in any way. It was just ... well, I think it was just free-floating malice. You see it everywhere these days and you saw it everywhere in those days too. Be that as it may, she leaned menacingly over the baby, raised a long bony finger, and uttered a terrible and fearful curse: "Oh yes, she has beauty, and, oh yes, she has virtue — but she will never be happy, because the man she falls in love with will never love her back!" Then, with the obligatory cruel cackle and puff of black smoke, she vanished.

Everybody gasped in horror! Then they said: But she *has* to be happy — one of the blessings was the gift of a happy disposition! And the King and the Queen wept; it seemed such a horrible curse to lay upon such a small baby. But after a while all the guests and the fairies assured the King and Queen that this Princess, so beautiful, so charming, so graceful, with all these wonderful virtues and gifts *would* be loved by everybody. So they calmed down a bit; and certainly, as time went on and as the Princess grew, and all the gifts came to be realized, it seemed to be true. Everybody *did* love her. She was so beautiful, so charming, so elegant, so graced with every virtue …

Young men — princes and kings and emperors — all came to court her. The Princess liked them all, but she didn't fall in love. Yet her manner was so winning and so charming that, although she turned them away, they went away loving her even more and vowing to return, should she but crook her little finger.

Well, the King and the Queen had long forgotten the curse. One day the Princess, who was now a beautiful young woman, was walking in the meadow and ahead of her she saw a young man, a Prince, grooming his horse. She walked closer to him, and she looked at him, and all of a sudden, she was smitten with love. Not that he was any different from any other of the princes or emperors or kings who had come courting her; but you know how it is, it's the chemistry of love — and this was it.

Now the Princess was used to success. She went over to him and she said, "Hello."

He turned to her and he said, "Hello." But in his eyes was not the look of a man in love. He did not seem to find the Princess so very extraordinary or interesting. But the Princess had no worries about it. First of all, she didn't know about the terrible curse that had been given to her when she was young; and second, she was *sure* of winning this young man's heart.

Every day she would go out to the meadow. Maybe one day she would sing a song in her delicate, beautiful voice. On another day she would come in a beautiful gown and dance. Or, on another day she would be walking with her friends, and he would see how charming and lovely she was with people. But although he seemed to *like* her well enough, he never fell in love.

Finally, after a few months of this, the princess came to the sad realization that he was not going to love her. He wasn't going to love her! Her heart was broken. She couldn't believe it. She'd never had a case of unrequited love in her whole life. Everybody who had ever met her had been entranced with her, and here was somebody who could take her or leave her, who could turn his back on her. So she did what all heroines do in a fairy tale. She lay down in the meadow and she wept. She wept, helpless and vulnerable, her heart broken.

And, since this is a fairy tale, a little, enchanted fairy in a blue dress heard her and appeared before her and said, "What's the matter?"

And the Princess told her story of loving this man who didn't love her back, and the fairy said, "I will give you three wishes. Choose them wisely, Princess."

The Princess smiled an enchanting smile. "One wish will do," she said. "I want that Prince," (she lowered her voice discreetly) "the one with the horse over there, to ..." (another enchanting smile) "love me."

The blue fairy gulped. This was her first assignment as a wish fairy and she wasn't thrilled about being the messenger of bad news. But she steeled herself, and told the Princess about the terrible curse. "You can ask your mother if you don't believe me," she said at the end. But the Princess didn't need to. One of her gifts was the ability to know the truth when she heard it and never need a second opinion.

"Do I still have three wishes?" she asked charmingly.

Remember — this Princess was also flexible and well-adjusted.

"Yes," said the blue fairy.

The Princess smiled. "Well, for my first wish, I wish for the power to be able to give him any gift in the world!" Suddenly she was able to give him — since he seemed to be interested in horses — a herd of the most magnificent white stallions. He liked the gift, but it didn't seem to bring on love. And she got him beautiful saddles and harnesses and splendid race tracks and courts and palaces and jewels ... One after the other, he accepted them and he was gracious; but he didn't fall in love with her.

So the Princess called upon the blue fairy again, and she said, "I'm ready for my second wish. I wish that I had the power to be any woman in the world!"

And so one day she would appear to the Prince delicate and petite — an Oriental woman with black shining hair and a little fan and a kimono. He was kind of interested, but he didn't fall in love. The next day she would appear blonde and willowy, and another day statuesque; until finally, after she had transformed herself into every kind of woman imaginable, and still he showed no interest, and still he went on doing what he had to do, grooming his horses and riding and not loving her, she went back to the meadow and she threw herself down on the ground and she wept.

The blue fairy reappeared and said, "You have one wish left. What is it to be?"

Now, you may remember that the name of this story is "The Third Wish." The Princess knew that, with only one wish left, she had to choose wisely and she had to choose well. And because this is a modern fairy tale I'm going to give you two possible endings. It's up to you. Ending number one:

The Princess, her heart heavy, a little bit cynical, a little bit wiser with sad experience, said: "All right ... let me not love him anymore!"

At that, she turned and she looked at the Prince, and he was now a man like all men, and she didn't love him anymore. She went back to her castle and with time she met all the other suitors who had come her way, and eventually she settled on one of them and she married him. Together they had a beautiful palace, near where her parents lived, and she had children, and she had grandchildren. And one day at a feast for one of her grandchildren, she saw the Prince — the Prince she had loved and suffered for and wept over. She saw him come in with his family and she saw him walk by; she saw him paunchy and balding and wrinkled; she looked at him and she said to herself, gathering her grandchildren around her and blessing her life — could *this* have been the man I sobbed for? And she counted herself lucky.

The second ending goes like this:

The third wish, thought the Princess — well, what is tormenting me is my love for him. I can't stop loving him but at least let it stop being an obsession! Let it stop being a torment! Let it just somehow *be* there, so that I can deal with it.

And so it was. She loved him, but she didn't feel *crazy* all the time. You know — that crazy feeling where if you're not with them and if you don't get them you're just going mad! That feeling went away.

The Prince noticed it. Now, you know how things are. When you're interested in somebody, they're not interested back. But when you're not so interested, then they do get interested. So the Prince turned and he began to notice her beautiful blonde curls and her big blue eyes, her long lashes, her delicate voice and all her winning ways — and he began to show an interest. He came around and he courted her, and eventually they were married.

Now, they had a castle near where her parents lived, and they had children, but there was a little problem. The Prince never understood why the Princess wasn't extraordinarily grateful — after all, she had been doing *everything* she could to get him, and now she had him and she seemed to be ... just content, not crazy with joy. He had expected she would absolutely worship the ground he walked on, and certainly not ever contradict him. She, on the other hand, was equally unhappy. She was, after all, a Princess who had been used to always getting her own way, to having people worship and adore her — and here was a man who sort of ... after a while ... agreed to marry her. She, who had had emperors and princes and kings court her! So she didn't understand why *he* didn't worship the ground she walked on.

They had children and they had grandchilren, and the marriage lasted until they died. And I'm not saying they weren't happy, but ... they had to work at it.

The Legend of Lady Meng

Frieda Ling

"I grew up on stories my grandmother told me —
adventurous stories of heroes and villains from Chinese
folklore; suspenseful stories of hapless princesses captured
by ferocious dragons; and noodle tales about dimwitted
sons-in-law. Unlike most women of her generation, my
grandmother could read quite well, although, as was
common in her day, she could not write much beyond her
own name. But when it comes to storytelling, I do not
believe the best storytellers of today can outshine her in
richness of repertoire or power of telling.

As much as I have wished to remember, I cannot
recall all the stories my grandmother told me. But I can
still see myself sitting on her bed in the tiny but
spotlessly clean mezzanine room that was hers or
sitting on the rooftop of our Shanghai duplex, begging
for more stories. Grandmother always obliged, after she
had exclaimed in her lilting Hangchow dialect, 'You little
child! Same stories again!' I would nod my head
vigorously and the stories would begin. That became
our daily ritual. One of my favourite stories is the one
that follows. I hope readers will enjoy the story and
come to love it as much as I have."

Along the Great Wall of China, near the Pass of Mountain and Ocean, stands a little temple. Inside is the solitary statue of a beautiful but plainly dressed young woman with a turban on her head. It is the statue of Lady Meng, a woman who dared to challenge the Emperor. Of all the stories that are told of the Great Wall, none is more poignant, tragic, and beautiful than the legend of Lady Meng. This is her story.

When Qin Shihuangti, First Sovereign Emperor of the mighty Middle Kingdom, decreed that the great walls were to be linked and expanded to ward off invasion of the northern barbarians, fear gripped all the able-bodied young men of the nation. Rich and poor, scholarly and uneducated, they were dragged off into eternal exile for the construction of the wall. The nation became drenched in tears of mourning — of old men and women for their sons, of young widows for their husbands, and of orphans for the fathers they would never see again.

Years went by. Tens of thousands of men were drafted to build the Great Wall; yet its completion was nowhere in sight. No sooner was a section erected than another fell down. In desperation, the Emperor sent for the Royal Diviner. His summons echoed down the marble corridors and carved stairways of the imperial palace.

The Royal Diviner, clad in priestly garb, was ushered in with ceremonial grandeur. From an incense urn he drew out a long thin slab inscribed with these words: "Human souls brave and pure/Each li needs to immure."

"Your Majesty, a wall this long can only be built if you immure a human being in every li of the wall," the Diviner explained. "Each li will then have its own guardian. Tens of thousands more men will have to die before your wall can be finished."

"Is there no other way?" the Emperor asked, not so much out of respect for human lives, which he regarded as cheap weeds, but out of a desire to simplify matters.

The Diviner thought long and hard. "There is, your Majesty," he replied after a long silence. "There are men by the rare name of Wan, which means 'ten thousand.' If only one of them can be recruited and sacrificed, further loss of innocent lives can be stopped. The construction can go on then without obstruction."

The Emperor was delighted with this brilliant solution. The hunt for young men of good repute by the name of Wan began immediately.

In the picturesque city of Suzhou there lived a young scholar by the name of Wan Shi-Liang. He panicked upon hearing the news of the hunt. Bidding a hasty good-bye to his parents, he ran away that same night, travelling in the opposite direction to the Great Wall, threading through back lancs and hidden alleys by day and crouching under bridges and in the undergrowth by night. He ran and ran, not daring to slow down, until one day he realized that his hair had grown long, his clothes were in shreds, and his toes no longer stayed inside his shoes. So changed was his appearance that he was beyond recognition.

One day, while he was walking along a country road, Wan heard with renewed fear the sound of galloping hooves. To his horror, he saw in the distance pennants of official recruiters. He immediately ran off the road and jumped over the first wall that he came to. He crouched close to the ground, not daring to breathe until he was sure the danger had passed.

When Wan finally lifted his head, he found himself in a most exquisite garden, flanked by majestic trees and adorned in the middle with a pond. Around the edge of the pond, a beautiful and richly dressed young woman was chasing butterflies. But as he watched with fascination behind the shrubs, he saw the young woman slip and fall into the water. He rushed from his hiding place, plunged into the pond, and carried her to safety.

"Who are you? How did you come in here?" asked the young woman. Her name was Meng Giang-Nu, and she was at once grateful for the rescue and shocked by the unexplained presence of the filth- and dust-covered vagabond.

"Please have pity on a fugitive, kind-hearted Miss. My name is Wan and I am on the run for my life from the Emperor's soldiers ... "

"Say no more, Squire Wan," Lady Meng cut short Wan's plea. "I understand."

Like everyone else, Lady Meng knew the story only too well. But now, face to face with sleepless eyes filled with sadness, a hollow voice full of despair, and a dirt-smeared face sallowed by fear, she was moved to tears by the plight of this hunted young man.

Meanwhile, the whole household had come out to see what the commotion was about. Lady Meng's parents were horrified to see this beggar-stranger carrying their daughter in his arms and shocked to notice the longing looks the young couple were casting at each other. In ancient days, unrelated young men and women were not allowed to see, let alone touch, each other.

"What is the meaning of this, daughter? Who is this beggar?" the alarmed parents cried out.

"Most venerable father and mother, please restrain your anger and hear me explain," begged Lady Meng. "If it were not for Squire Wan, I would have drowned because of my own carelessness. Please let him stay — to repay him for saving my life."

At the mention of the name "Wan," the parents knew what had brought Wan to their doorsteps. On learning that Wan was from a good family, they felt greatly relieved and allowed the marriage of their daughter to take place without delay. And, with the life of a fugitive far behind him, Wan settled down to a happy life with his wife and his in-laws.

But, as the ancient saying goes, good fortune never lasts. Such a story was too good to escape gossipy tongues and before long it travelled all the way to the local magistrate. An arrest warrant was issued for the man with the fatal name. Soldiers came one night, seized Wan, and took him away.

Not one day passed when Lady Meng did not think of her ill-fated husband. She hoped against hope that somehow, miraculously, he would escape the cruel fate awaiting him. With loving care, she quilted a coat of padded cotton and, when the first winds of autumn filled her pond with floating leaves, she persuaded her parents to let her deliver the coat in person.

So it was that Lady Meng, who had led a sheltered life, embarked on a dangerous journey of thousands of li in search of her husband. After many months of treading through icy mountains and fording treacherous waters, she came to the place where the wall was being built. But it was already too late.

"Everyone remembers your husband well — the one who was supposed to take the place of thousands of others," the foreman shook his head sadly as he recalled what happened. "He was so frail and so frightened. I could tell by one look that he was not the labouring kind. He died in a matter of weeks. Come, I will take you to the pavilion where he was buried in the foundation of the wall."

When Lady Meng came to where Wan was buried, she sank to her knees and began to cry. For seven days and seven nights she wept. She wept for the love she had for her husband, she wept for the pain they had gone through, and she wept for the suffering the evil Emperor had imposed on others. So powerful and intense were her tears, legend has it that at the end of the seventh day the earth trembled, the pillars of the pavilion collapsed, and the roof caved in to reveal the bones of the dead.

News of this miraculous happening spread like fire until it reached the Emperor, who was inspecting the work nearby. Qin Shihaugnti was incensed. He had Lady Meng summoned to him immediately.

"Who are you, prisoner woman, that you dare disturb the progress of imperial construction?" the Emperor thundered.

Lady Meng was not intimidated, though her hands were bound tight behind her back and her head was pressed low by the cold edge of the swords held by the soldiers who flanked her. Feeling a righteous anger surging inside her, she replied, "Thousands of men have died because of you. May you, who have robbed innocent men of their lives, never know peace in life or repose in death!"

"Remove her for immediate execution!" roared the Emperor, his shout thundering down the make-shift court he had set up near the Wall. But just as the soldiers were dragging Lady Meng away, the Emperor caught a glimpse of her face. He was astounded to see how young and beautiful she was. In a changed tone he said, "You are indeed a woman of exceptional courage. I will grant you all of your heart's desires if you will come to the palace with me."

Everyone, from the lowliest slave boy to the highest-ranking official, waited breathlessly for Lady Meng's answer. To everyone's surprise, she replied, "I consent — but only upon three conditions."

"Name your conditions and they shall be done," promised the Emperor, without the slightest hesitation.

"First, you must build a magnificent tomb by the River Yangtze for my husband."

"It shall be built according to your specifications."

"Second, I request a terrace forty-nine feet high beside the tomb in memory of my husband."

"It shall be erected to your satisfaction."

"Third, you yourself, O Most Supreme Emperor, must officiate at the burial of my husband and mourn him as a son mourns his father."

"This I cannot do," the Emperor began to say. But Lady Meng looked so beautiful even in mourning that the Emperor swallowed his pride and agreed to all three conditions.

When the time came for Wan to be buried, Lady Meng and Qin Shihuang arrived dressed in the deepest mourning. The Emperor officiated at the most elaborate of rituals for the departed soul of Wan. When the ceremonies were over, the Emperor beckoned to Lady Meng and said, "Come, change into the silk embroidered gowns I have prepared for you. We shall celebrate our wedding feast."

Instead, before anyone could stop her, Lady Meng ran to the top of the terrace and cursed the Emperor for his cruelty in a loud and defiant voice: "The Great Wall will be powerless against the barbarians, but you, you who are more heartless than the lowest of beasts, will be hated forever by generations to come!"

At that, Lady Meng jumped into the torrential waters of the Yangtse River and was seen no more.

Many years later the curse of Lady Meng came true. The empire of Qin Shihuangti collapsed shortly after his death.

The Great Wall, impressive as it was, failed to keep out the ferocious Tartars who, under Genghis Khan, Universal Ruler of all the Mongols, swooped down on flying horses across the northern plains and conquered China. Qin Shihuangti has come down in history as the most despicable of Chinese emperors. The memory of the courageous Lady Meng, on the other hand, is honoured and cherished even to this day.

The Legend of Lupi the Great White Wolf

Esther Jacko

"I am an Ojibway storyteller from the Whitefish River First Nation, which is located in Birch Island, Ontario. I was privileged to learn about the Ojibway Nation's history, and in particular the history of my tribe within that Nation, while I was growing up on my Reserve. My grandparents Bill and Annie Migwanabi imparted this history to me through the traditional art of storytelling.

I always looked forward to listening to a recital of our tribe's movements, battles for territory, accounts of their losses and victories, and where the enemy was buried. I particularly enjoyed stories about thunders, winds and nature in general and how our ancestors were always with us even though they had passed from us. I learned from an early age who I was, where I fit in, and what my overall purpose was in relation to my tribe's continuity and survival.

I was able to come to a knowledge and development of this through my exposure to my history and its teachings. Ojibway beliefs, values, customs and traditions of long ago were woven into my upbringing to help me understand what I needed to know to live a way of life practised for generations upon the land, and to share the value of that with others.

I have been fortunate in having the opportunity to share what I have learned with my children, and I am grateful that circle has widened to include a greater audience. I am often invited into the local schools in our area to relate what I know to the children there. I feel they should be exposed to storytelling as a method of teaching because it is so warm, enjoyable and entertaining. What an absolutely perfect way to learn about their local history. Sometimes we take the children right to historical sites and relate the legends to them from the spots where it all happened. It is wonderful to see their imagination and thoughts stimulated by these kinds of visits.

My Grandpa Bill shared the story of *Lupi the Great White Wolf* with my Grandma Annie, who shared it with me when I asked her to explain to me why our tribe left their ancestral island and moved to the mainland.

I learned many lessons from this story, such as our people's way of life in everyday situations while they lived on the Island. I became acquainted with the traditions that were supposed to be kept regarding marriage and the betrothal, the importance of dreams, family and feelings, to name a few. I also learned about the importance of forgiveness, the tragedy of vengeance, and the eternity of love.

Grandma is very proud that Grandpa's voice and a piece of our history will reach out so far to so many people through being included in this book. I am both happy and proud as well, to play my small role in writing it all down to help make this possible.

Storytelling is an art and tradition that must be shared continually through the spoken word. *Lupi the Great White Wolf* is meant to be spoken from one person to another, so do not be shy, find an eager listener and share this story with them. In this way you will experience the way it was always meant to be shared, through the warmth of the human voice. Enjoy yourselves as it comes to life for each of you personally."

▼▼▼

This story began on a large Island known as Wha-wha-skin-ah-gah, which is the Ojibway name for Birch Island. It is located in a huge bay of waters, which today is called Mc-Gregor Bay. This story is about a tribe of Ojibway people who lived on this Island long, long ago in days gone by. These people were part of a great Nation of Ojibway that occupied the largest area of land on what we know as Turtle Island, or North America.

This particular tribe of Ojibway were proud that their Island sat in the centre of a busy trade route. Their Island was completely surrounded by large waters, so they could always see who was passing by or coming over. Anyone travelling from the East had to pass this Island to get through to the West. It was a very strategic location.

In those days the Ojibway people were well known for being trappers and traders. The Ojibway men were excellent hunters and fishers as well. The men of the tribe were always busy in these activities and the women of the tribe were always busy along with them.

The men trapped luxuriant mink and beaver for their furs, which the women prepared into fine pelts. The men hunted deer for food and skins and the Ojibway women prepared these skins until they were soft and supple and then fashioned them into the finest of clothing and moccasins. The women spent long months decorating these items with quillwork in unusual and beautiful designs. The men caught plenty of fish that the women would salt and smoke. Birchbark and black ash were gathered from trees and made into strong and useful baskets. The women harvested maple tree sap in the spring and made syrup, sugar cakes and pull taffy. They also gathered berries and fruits, and herbs and medicines from plants, then packed them into baskets after drying them.

All of these items were used every day by the Ojibways, but they were also used for trade with other tribes. When the women planted corn, squash, beans and potatoes, the men would travel great distances to trade their goods. When they returned they brought medicines, herbs and salt from faraway places, because these things could not be found on their island. Pipestone, copper and silver metal, clay cooking vessels and rare dyes were just some of the prized items they would bring back.

There was another unique feature about this Island, in addition to its strategic location and the industrious people who lived there. On this Island lived a young maiden. Her Ojibway name was Nungoose, which means Little Star, and she was the most beautiful girl anyone had ever seen. Her laughter was like a bubbling brook, and her smile was like a morning sunrise. When she danced, she was as graceful as a deer. And when Nungoose sang, everyone would stop to listen, her voice was so sweet and melodious. Of course you can imagine that she had many admirers from near and far.

At the time when this story begins, Nungoose's father, who was the great Chief of the tribe, had announced that he would be hearing proposals for her hand in marriage.

In those days it was customary for the prospective groom to make an offer of a dowry directly to the Chief. This dowry would be offered for the favour of the daughter's hand. The Chief usually acknowledged the biggest dowry and awarded his daughter's hand in marriage accordingly. This served two purposes. It made the Chief richer, and it gave the family an idea of what kind of provider the groom would be.

Nungoose had many admirers who busied themselves trying to get her attention. The young men would perform all sorts of antics in front of her. Some would wrestle, some would race one another to prove how strong or fast they were. Some would climb high trees to prove to her that they were not afraid. Nungoose and her friends were amused by these competitions for a while, and when they grew tired of them, they would retreat to their secret place and talk about how funny the young men looked when they fell out of a tree, or tripped in a race and went rolling. Nungoose and her friends would enjoy a merry laugh over it all.

There were many young men who sought out Nungoose's attention in an aggressive way. This put Nungoose off because she was a gentle person.

There was, however, someone Nungoose truly liked. But he, unlike the others, had shown no interest in her, and she could not understand this. She loved to listen as he played the flute that he had whittled himself. His Ojibway name was Nimki, which means Little Thunder, and he was handsome and strong.

Nungoose would watch Nimki working hard at his father's side. She would hide in her secret place to watch him swim; he was so strong and fast and beautiful to watch. She made up her mind to find out how he felt about her. She could stand it no longer, not knowing …

For his part, Nimki had watched the other boys, as he liked to refer to them, making fools of themselves in front of Nungoose. I am a man, he thought to himself. He did not need to resort to play to get Nungoose's attention. He worshipped Nungoose and wanted her for his wife, and he worked long hours every day to prepare a dowry to win her. He was not sure how Nungoose felt about him, though. She did not seem to be interested in anyone from the village. Nimki worried that her affections were being reserved for someone else, someone not from their Island. Each time he would sneak glances at her, and she would catch his eye, he would quickly look away. It frustrated Nimki that he could not show his feelings. Sometimes he thought Nungoose was watching him, but when he caught her eye, she in turn would quickly look away. Nimki just did not know what to think, and the time was drawing near for the Chief to hear the proposals.

Finally, the time for the proposals approached. That very night, at the start of the Spring Ceremonies, the Chief would set the final date. This made Nimki all the more nervous. He paced and he pondered on what he should do.

Meanwhile, Nungoose prepared herself for the evening's festivities. Tonight her father would announce the date when he expected all dowry offers to be made. Her mother had told her that she would be married and in her own lodge by summer. Nungoose was worried that she would end up with one of the young, foolish men, or worse, a stranger from afar. Her heart pined away for Nimki, and she whispered secret prayers: "Oh Nimki, when will you notice me?"

Later on that evening Nungoose found herself sitting at one of the ceremonial fires, in front of Nimki. Most everyone else was dancing, and Nungoose and Nimki began to stare at one another. Such longing was exchanged in their gazes. Suddenly Nungoose felt a wood chip hit her lap. She picked it up and looked at Nimki, then threw it back to him. Nimki picked up the wood chip once again and threw it into Nungoose's lap. Nungoose picked it up and threw it back.

The Chief sat at a distance and observed this exchange, and to his wife he said, "I was getting worried about those two, but my suspicions are correct; they are very much in love. The dowry settlement should prove interesting indeed."

"What are you saying?" asked Nungoose's mother. "Tradition says the man with the largest dowry wins! Are you saying that you will give your daughter's hand for love?"

The Chief looked at his wife and smiled, "I am not saying anything, just making an observation." His wife understood — if anyone could change tradition, it was her husband, the Chief.

Later on that evening the Chief announced that he would begin hearing dowry proposals by the end of the next full moon.

Off to the side of the circle sat Nimki and Nungoose, holding each other's hands tenderly. "Oh Nimki," sighed Nungoose, "I thought you would never notice me …"

"I have noticed you all along, Nungoose, ever since we were children," Nimki said. "Your father had announced the time when he will receive dowry proposals, and I must get back to my work in preparing one which will win you. I will not see you again until that day. I will not fail, Nungoose, you will be my wife."

Before he turned to leave, Nimki gave Nungoose his flute. Nungoose kissed his cheek and said, "I will pledge myself to no other, and I will await your return, Nimki. Hurry back to me."

As Nimki rushed home to tell his parents the news, he felt tall and mighty. He would show the great Chief that he was worthy indeed. He would produce the best dowry possible.

Nungoose rushed to see her mother. "Oh, mother," she cried, "I am in love and it feels wonderful! Tonight Nimki pledged himself to me!"

"Ah! Daughter, do not be hasty, your father is the one who will decide who your husband is to be."

Nungoose knelt down beside her mother and pleaded, " Speak to my father, plant a seed in his heart."

"Yes, daughter," Nungoose's mother said. She held her daughter near, and thought back to the time when her own heart had been captured.

In time, the big day arrived. Many young men made their way into the centre of the village. After choosing their spots they began to pile up their goods, going back and forth to their lodges for items they had left behind. Suddenly there were shouts from the eastern shore of the Island, which was near the village. "Someone new has arrived! Come everyone, come see the strangers."

Everyone dropped what they were doing to go down to the shore. The Chief was curious about the reaction the strangers had aroused in his people. After all, several suitors had already arrived this way — what was so different about these newcomers?

As the Chief turned the final bend in the trail that led down to the shore, he stopped suddenly. He could not believe his eyes. An old woman and young man were climbing out of the lead canoe, and behind them followed helpers with ten large canoes filled with goods of all kinds. Some of the helpers unpacked a few of the bundles to remove choice items and display them before the Chief. They brought forward ceremonial masks and rattles carved out of wood. The crowd of onlookers gasped as the masks were raised high for all to see. Finely decorated buffalo robes and strands of highly prized wampum were displayed next: slowly they were turned so the Chief could carefully inspect them. The Chief's heart began to pound as the helpers packed away the goods.

"Great Chief," the old woman said at last, "I have come today to offer you this dowry on behalf of my grandson, so that he may have your daughter's hand in marriage."

Silence fell suddenly amongst the chattering tribespeople. A foreboding mood settled over the crowd: who was this strange woman, and where did she come from? No one could tell which tribe she came from. Her dress and accent were unusual, yet she knew how to speak the Ojibway language.

"Let your grandson speak for himself," said the Chief.

"He cannot speak," said the old woman. "He has been that way since his early childhood. I will speak for him. Look: he has worked hard to gather this dowry. Many times he has passed your way during his trading voyages, and he has noticed your fair daughter. He desires her for his wife. Can you not see he will provide well for her and make you a rich man also?"

The Chief did not trust this woman or her grandson; there was something mysterious and disturbing about their presence. He decided he would give himself some time to make his decision.

"I will consider your offer with the rest," said the Chief. "You may wait here, or on the nearby island across the way. It may take me longer than expected to make a decision, there are so many offers."

"Very well," said the old woman, "but do not keep us waiting long. We have a great distance to travel when this is all over." The helpers slowly turned the heavy canoes around and pointed them in the direction of the nearby island where they would make their camp.

The Chief was worried as he started back up the path to the village. This old woman and her grandson intended to take his dear daughter far, far away. He was also worried for another reason. The largest dowry dictated who his choice should be — that was tradition.

Nungoose ran down the path toward her father. She had seen everything. Grabbing her father by the arm, she pleaded with him in a tender soft voice, tears welling in her eyes: "Please do not give me to this strange man as a wife. He frightens me so. It is Nimki that I love, dear father. I shall die without him!"

The Chief looked at his fair child. Her eyes reminded him of a wounded doe in the forest. His heart was filled with compassion and he embraced his child.

Nimki, too, had witnessed the scene at the shore, and he grew very troubled. He had worked hard to gather his dowry, but it could not compare with that of the old woman and her grandson. Yet his heart was strong in its love for Nungoose. I must try! he thought to himself. If my dowry does not work I will give it away and take Nungoose and escape to a place where we cannot be found!

After spending the day receiving proposals, the Chief retired into his lodge to rest and make his decision. "Oh, wife," he said, "what am I to do? No one has brought a larger dowry than the old woman."

His wife said, "No one has brought a larger dowry, but I noticed someone who brought one better in quality!"

The Chief looked at his wife and said, "Nimki has worked very hard! If it had not been for the old woman, I could have chosen Nimki; but tradition states I must give my daughter to the one who offers the largest dowry."

"What a foolish tradition!" said the wife. "It should be changed. Some tradiitons can make people so unhappy! You are a great Chief, you can change this tradition. You will not lose the respect of your people. You will gain further respect instead by recognizing not only the dowry of goods, but the dowry of love. Show your people your heart and its humility."

The Chief embraced his wife and said, "You are my heart and wisdom, and you are right. Go out and call the people together."

So the great Chief announced his decision and gave his reasons for bypassing tradition and refusing the dowry offered by the old woman on behalf of her grandson.

"I will accept the offer of Nimki," said the Chief. "In this way I will make my daughter happy and our tribe will not lose its fair flower." Everyone whooped and cheered after hearing this good news. "Let the wedding begin!" they cried.

As Nungoose was dressing in her finest array, someone called in at the entrance to her parents' lodge. "Nungoose, it is I, Nimki — may I come in?" Nungoose stood up and straightened herself. She was ready. Nimki walked over to her and in his hands he carried a string of wampum. Wampum was a very valuable item because a lot of work went into producing it. Purple-white shells were gathered from the sea, ground by hand and shaped into cylindrical and circular disks. Delicate and skilled handiwork was required to turn these shells into a finished product. As well, a high value was placed on wampum because it had to be obtained through trade and because it was used to keep records or agreements which were considered sacred. Presenting a woman with marriage wampum was the way a prospective groom pledged himself to his future wife. "These are for you," Nimki said, as he placed the wampum over Nungoose's head so the shells could drape her neck. "Let this strand always remind you of our love, and how eternal it shall be, like the circle."

Nungoose gasped! No other woman in the tribe possessed such a valuable article. Some had the beginnings of a strand, in pouches they wore at their sides. It took many furs to trade for a handful. Usually a woman waited a long time to have such a complete strand. Nungoose felt so proud!

"I will place a new strand next to this one when our first child is born," Nimki said. "After our wedding I must leave to trade, so you can have everything you need for our lodge."

"Oh Nimki, please stay," Nungoose pleaded.

"I will need the good weather on my side. We will be together all winter," Nimki replied. "Come Nungoose, they are waiting for us. Let us marry and feast and enjoy this great day!" And so out they went to celebrate their love with their people.

While preparations for the wedding got underway, the Chief sent a messenger to give news of his decision to the old woman and her grandson on the nearby Island. Upon receiving the message, the old woman stood up abruptly, spat on the ground and said, "Tell your great Chief I do not accept this news. He will live to regret it!"

While night fell and the full moon rose, the old woman hatched her plot of revenge. "Grandson," she called, "come sit here by the fire with me. I will tell you a story.

"We are all that is left of our tribe," the old woman began. "When you were a baby, an attack was led against us by that Chief over there on the next Island. He and his men destroyed everything. The Chief does not remember me, I was younger then, but it was I who begged him to spare your life. As he rode by, he dropped you next to me, and your head struck the ground. I think that is why you cannot speak to this day.

"I sought to amend my grief over this by taking his dear daughter to be your wife. Now he has given her to another.

"But he will not have his way," she said. "Nungoose will be yours. You will see, all you have to do is co-operate with me. Go over there and unwrap that bundle and bring it to me ..."

The grandson did as he was told, and uncovered white furs and a wolf's dried-up head.

"Do you want Nungoose for yourself?" the old woman asked her grandson. The grandson nodded his head. "Then wrap yourself in these skins and lay by the fire. I have medicine which will transform you into a most fearsome animal, and then back into a man if you wish. You will have speech and great power too, for I will use my medicine songs to change the wrongs that have been done to you."

The old woman knew that she was not supposed to use these medicines to her advantage, but she stubbornly went ahead. She had been warned that these powers, if misused, could be harmful and bounce back upon her. Ah, but her feelings of revenge were stronger than the warnings.

All through the night the old woman chanted and sang. She threw her medicines into the fire with a vengeance. Great thunder and lightning flashed and rumbled and roared. The Creator was displeased, she knew, but tossing her cares to the strong, heavy winds, she sang higher and higher, until the night sky exploded with one thunderous roar!

Suddenly everything grew quiet. The old woman stared at the form beginning to stir. Then, over the dying embers of the fire there sprang a great white wolf. He lifted his head, and his howl filled the predawn air. Lupi the great white wolf had been born! Quickly the old woman helped him into a canoe, and swiftly she paddled him to Wha-wha-skin-ah-gah. They landed there in the early hours of the morning, and slipped like shadows into the deep forest.

Later on that morning the people remarked to one another about the fierce storm that had passed overhead the night before. "Very strange that there was no rain," one said. "I thought I heard the howl of a very large wolf," said another one.

Nungoose and Nimki had spent their first night together as husband and wife. As they stood outside on this fine morning they were not aware of the danger that lurked nearby, nor did they pay any attention to the chatter of the other tribe members. They held hands and walked down to the shore. Nimki would leave in three days and he wanted to spend as much time with Nungoose as he could.

Those three days passed quickly and Nimki prepared to leave, promising Nungoose that he would not be long. "I will bring you back something special!" he called. Then he gave her a wave and he was gone.

Life returned to normal in the small village, or so it seemed. The people were not aware that Lupi watched their comings and going. He grew hungrier and hungrier and paced back and forth, until he could no long restrain himself. It was then he decided to select his first victim and, without remorse, Lupi began to stalk him.

Later that day, at sunset, some of the young men were returning from a day of fishing. They unloaded their canoes and prepared their catch into bundles. "Our mothers will be proud," they said to one another. "Let us start home quickly," and up the trail they disappeared.

The last young man in line stopped momentarily, and laid down his bundle so he could rest. He was tired from the big day. The forest was quiet now, the birds had stopped chirping. He picked up his bundle and decided to run to catch up with the rest of his quickly disappearing friends. Then he heard a feeble voice calling out, "My son, help me!" The young man dropped his bundle and began to search off the trail, wandering back and forth amongst the trees. Behind two large trees he discovered an Elder who had fallen down. His leg was twisted underneath him.

"Help me, my son, I am hurt," said the Elder. The young man rushed over and put his arms around the old man to lift him. Suddenly he felt the old man's arms grip him with a strength he had never before felt. The young man straightened himself to see if the old one had recovered; and he found himself staring into the jaws of a huge white wolf. Overcome with fear, he let out a bloodcurdling yell. His friends up the trail stopped momentarily; then they laughed to one another and said, "Our friend tries to fool us." So they yelled back, and kept going.

The sound of their voices drowned out the wolf's gnashing jaws as he ripped his first victim apart and ate him.

Much later that evening, the mother of the young man inquired of his friends as to his whereabouts.

"Why, is he not home yet?" asked one. "We thought he was tricking us on the way back." Then the father returned with his missing son's bundle, which he had found abandoned on the trail. "I am very concerned," he said, "I feel something has happened to my son."

The Chief formed a search party. He cautioned the men to stay in pairs, and as close together as possible. Then off into the night they went.

One pair of young men were walking together, having just left the village. "Psst, psst," a whisper drifted over to one of them. The young man looked up, and there on the rise of a knoll, peeking out from behind a tree, was a young village woman he admired very much. She must have followed me, he thought to himself. I will send her back. Not wanting his friend to know of this encounter, he said to him, "My friend, why not go down this slope?" and he pointed up and added, "I will go up this way to check."

"But brother," the friend replied, "the Chief told us not to separate."

"We are brave and strong, it will not hurt us to separate for a moment," his friend said. "Besides we will save time this way." His friend accepted this explanation and started down the hill, calling back over his shoulder, "Only for a moment, brother!"

The young man rushed up the hill. Oh, he would scold her all right, take some kisses, too — oh, just wait until I get my hands on her, he thought to himself! The young man found the young woman giggling behind the tree. "Come here," he said. "There's something I want to show you!" He scooped her up in his arms and pressed himself against her and thought, I will be more than a moment, brother. It was dark where they were hidden, so he nuzzled around searching for her lips.

Suddenly the young man heard a low rumble coming from the woman's throat and her arms gripped him with an unusual strength. Foul breath came down upon him as he stared, shocked, into the jaws of a huge white wolf! There was no time for him to scream. With one snap of his powerful jaws Lupi had taken another victim. The young man's body rolled down the small hill, making small thumping noises. His friend, who was waiting in the shadows, stepped out to greet him, just as the headless friend came to rest at his feet.

"Help, help!" screamed the young friend. "Somebody help … !"

The other searchers came upon a grisly mess; fear gripped their hearts as they wondered what kind of creature could have inflicted such damage. "Let us return to the village, it is not safe here anymore for any of us," they said to one another. So they gathered up their brother's remains and set out on their way.

The women prepared the young man's body for cremation. The Chief stood before it and said, "This is the fate that must have met the young man who has gone missing. From now on I must warn you to stay together in strong groups. You must not separate!"

In the days that followed this event, all the men of the village stopped their work to become watchmen, some sleeping while others kept watch and then switching roles when they awoke. In this way they protected the village.

Gradually, whatever had threatened the tribe seemed to be gone, and slowly the people began to relax. One day a group of children were chasing some rabbits and off they scattered in all directions. Their mothers became alarmed that the children were entering the woods and chased after them. Those in the village chuckled at such a display: yes, indeed, things were back to normal.

One by one, the children and mothers all disappeared that day, never to return. Lupi would turn himself into a child and cry out for the mother, then he would turn himself into a mother and cry out to the child. In this wicked way they all died.

When the people of the village realized what had happened, they were filled with a terrible fear. "Great Chief, what shall we do to protect ourselves from this unseen force?" they cried. The Chief asked his Elders to fast and pray for an answer, and he also fasted and prayed.

During the third night of fasting, Lupi and the old woman appeared to the Chief in a dream. "Give us Nungoose," they demanded. The old woman said, "Look at my grandson now, how great and powerful he is. Each time he eats a human being he grows larger and more fearsome. Give us your daughter and we will leave your people alone!"

"No," cried the Chief in his dream, "You are evil, I will never hand my daughter over to you!"

In the Chief's dream, Lupi jumped on him and said, "Then I will eat you and everyone else, until only Nungoose is left!" This same night a Waterbird appeared to one of the Elders in a dream. "Tell your Chief to take his people and leave Wha-wha-skin-ah-gah, or Lupi will devour you all!"

"The wolf will follow us," the wise Elder replied.

"He will follow you, but only to the shore; if he goes into the water he will burn up."

"How can the water burn him?" asked the Elder.

"We have asked the Creator to place his powers into the waters surrounding your Island to help protect you from this evil," the Waterbird said. "Awaken, Elder, and tell your great Chief."

The Elder and Chief came out of their lodges together and spoke to one another about their dreams.

It was early morning as they began to awaken the people. "Rise up, pack what belongings you can take, we must leave here before Lupi destroys us all!" The Chief watched sadly as his people made haste. They would have to leave their ancestral home to rid themselves of this scourge.

"Father," cried Nungoose, "we cannot leave. Who will Nimki have to come back to?"

"I will send messengers ahead, dear daughter. We will be able to tell him where to find us," said the Chief.

Nungoose began to pack what belongings she could take. She had awakened so quickly that morning, she hoped that she would not forget something important amongst her possessions.

The people were rushing about and down to the shore to load their canoes. Some were already sitting down in the canoes, waiting to leave. The Chief looked across to the mainland. Somewhere on that shore, they would have to make their new home.

Nungoose settled herself into her canoe. People were pushing away and beginning to leave, while others were still coming down to the shore. It was such confusion to have to flee their home in this way. Oh Nimki, thought Nungoose as she raised her hand to her neck, I wish you were here. "What

... where is my wampum necklace?" Nungoose had reached up to reassure herself by touching Nimki's gift. She searched her bundle. "It's not there!" In a panic she jumped from the canoe and ran up the trail. She had to find her precious wampum necklace — to leave it behind would never do.

The Chief did not miss Nungoose until it was too late. "Nungoose, Nungoose," he called.

Nungoose had already hurried up the path before she realized that she was completely alone. Where were all the people who had been running back and forth? She grew anxious as she began to search the ground. She knew that she should not be alone.

There! There was her wampum necklace hanging on a branch! She had forgotten to put it on that morning because of the rush. She reached up and pulled it off the tree, then spun around to run. She could hear her father calling her.

Suddenly a handsome man appeared on the trail. "Nungoose, where are you off to? Do not leave, stay here with me, I will protect you. If you do not like me I will change my looks. I can be more handsome than this," he said. Right before her eyes he transformed again and again. This hypnotized Nungoose. The man's soothing voice mesmerized her. He reached for her and the wampum necklace she was holding fell to the ground. This broke the spell. Nungoose reached down, then pushed past this handsome man and began to run.

"Come back here!" he demanded, and started to chase her. Nungoose ran faster. She looked over her shoulder and saw the largest white wolf that could ever be. He was as big as five bears! Suddenly, just as the canoes came into view, she tripped.

As Nungoose fell she struck her head upon a rock. Lupi pounced over her only to hear her whisper, "I love you, Nimki," with her dying breath.

This enraged Lupi and he let out a howl. There in the water, standing in a canoe, the Chief was shouting, "Nungoose, Nungoose get up!" Now the Chief was the object of Lupi's revenge. If the Chief had given him Nungoose she would still be alive! Convinced of this, he tore down the path towards the lake. What a fearsome sight he made, charging towards the screaming people.

"Push out! Out!" commanded the Chief. They were in deep waters now. Lupi sprang into the water towards them, and then he began to burn. The people watched, horrified, as his fur caught flame. Howling in pain, he made his way back to the shore. He dragged himself up and rolled in the sand. The smell of burning fur and flesh filled the air. From the woods, the old woman called him to herself. Lupi limped towards her, and then passed out.

The Chief was filled with sadness as he watched Nungoose's still form. He would settle the people and return for her body. When at last the tribe landed on the mainland, he fell down, broken-hearted and weeping.

The following morning, while the villagers slept, Nimki alighted on the shore of his home. The messenger had missed him. He walked up the trail thinking how much he missed Nungoose. He would surprise her by taking this back trail.

Now Nimki saw what looked like Nungoose and her Grandmother picking berries. There was something unusual about the old woman, he thought. "Nungoose!" he called out. "It is me, your husband. I have returned."

Nungoose jumped up and ran towards Nimki with great speed. What has happened? thought Nimki. She has never run this fast before! Then, in front of his eyes Nimki saw Nungoose transform herself into a great white wolf.

Nimki barely had time to draw his knife, as Lupi sprang and knocked him down. Nimki fought strongly, letting out loud warrior whoops when he plunged his knife in. The people on the mainland were awakened by the sounds of this great struggle. Alas, Nimki's knife could not find its mark, and Lupi plunged his fangs into Nimki's throat.

"He has died an honorable death," whispered the Chief to those standing next to him. Now his own pain and his loss were doubled.

Back on the island, the old woman spoke to her grandson and said, "You have done well. We played here to win Nungoose for your own, and though we lost her, I have won my revenge! Cheer up, grandson, we will now leave this place. Come, we will search and we will find a far better maiden." But, as they prepared to leave, a Waterbird suddenly appeared and spoke to the old woman: "The Creator sends a message that he is displeased. You must leave your grandson behind, he will never be a man again after this. You will leave Old Woman, for your punishment is to walk the remainder of your days alone. Your grandson will stay here forever, for what he has done."

"No, no, no!" cried the Old Woman, but it was done. Her plan of revenge had backfired.

This legend ends happily and shows that true love can overcome the greatest evil. Fifty years ago, fishers visiting the waters around the island reported an interesting scene. While fishing in the quiet morning hours, their boat drifted in and out of the lake mists. They heard the gentle and sweet singing of a young woman. They paddled closer to the island to get a closer look and heard the laughter of a young man. As their boat left the northern shadow of the island and faced the East, they saw the sunrise beam down through the mists. There, walking hand in hand, they saw a beautiful maiden and a young handsome man, singing and laughing as they walked along ...

The fishers reported what they had seen to the owners of the Lodge where they were staying. The Lodge owners asked the Elders of our community what this could mean. "Oh, that is Nungoose and Nimki," one Elder answered. "Their love is eternal and so strong that sometimes they appear near the home they loved. Those were their spirits you have seen."

To this day, some people report hearing a haunting melody coming from the island; but when they search they cannot find the woman who sings it for them. And some nights, when people pass this island on their journeys, they say they hear the lonesome howling of a wolf. The Elders say that these are reminders to us of what happened there so long ago.

This story explains the migration of my Ojibway tribe from Wha-wha-skin-ah-gah to their settlement on the mainland, which today carries the name Birch Island. And now if someone asks you why they call Birch Island by that name, when it is not an island at all, you can share the Legend of Lupi the Great White Wolf with them.

Hauntings

Voiceover

From our first game of Peek-a-boo, we humans are prone to believe that what's hidden from sight is just as fascinating as the visible world. In the stories that follow, you'll meet many visitors from the world beyond the everyday. Some have been told about for over a thousand years by Native storytellers. Others have come to Canada with the immigrants from other countries.

Some ghosts are frightening, some are benevolent. In Alexander Wolfe's Saulteaux family history, the spirit of a dead grandfather protects his grandson. The Maemaegawaehnse is also a kindly spirit, playing with a boy who has lost his mother. Then there are the scary ghosts. Our northern forest is haunted by the Loup-Garou and Feu-Follet; the waters off the Gaspé are haunted by the ghosts of Blanche and the other French women who chose to die rather than stay on board the pirate ship; and on a certain stretch of lonely road on the west coast you may meet a young woman striving desperately to go back home. Give her a ride, as Nan Gregory did, and you'll have a story to ell your grandchildren. You'll also meet two remarkable real-life women from the Maritimes: Maggie Lochlin, who could "read" the weather; and the doomed Christine, the "Lady in the Snow," who braved a New Brunswick blizzard to try to save her children.

167

The Loup-Garou and the Shawl
Marylyn Peringer

"There are a few things you should know about the loup-garou. He (in French Canada it's almost always a man) prowls even when the moon's not full, unlike his English cousin. Sometimes he's out in the daytime. He's not necessarily in the shape of a wolf, or even a large dog — though he often is. Occasionally (as in this story) his form isn't specified, so the listener must imagine one. I've discovered loup-garou stories involving pigs, cows, horses, once even a Canada goose.

And why should this horrible transformation be inflicted on anyone? Not, as you might think, from being bitten by another loup-garou. No, in French Canada there was only one cause: a seven-year failure to fulfill one's 'Easter duty' of receiving the sacrament of Holy Communion at Easter time, a practice which was obligatory for Catholics in good standing."

There was once a married couple, Luc and Marie-Rose, and they lived near the edge of the forest. Now Luc had not been to church for seven years: even at Eastertime, he had not taken communion from the priest. So, of course, he began to run loup-garou. Every night he left the house, went into the forest, and would not come home till morning.

And he did not run alone. There was a whole pack of them, and they always ran in single file, a line of wild animals. There were ten of them, and since Luc was the last to join the pack, he was always the tenth, last in line.

Marie-Rose, his wife, knew nothing. She knew that her husband was never home at night, but she didn't know what was really happening. Every time she asked about his absences, he became cross and unpleasant; he answered her with silence, rudeness, or lies. Finally she stopped asking questions.

Late one afternoon, Marie-Rose found that her supply of kindling was low, so she went out into the forest to gather firewood. To carry it home, she brought her big shawl, an old one, made of thick wool woven in an Indian pattern of red and yellow. She knotted the opposite corners about her neck, throwing twigs and fallen branches into the shawl as she went along. So intent was she on her thoughts that she did not notice the time passing. By the time her shawl was full to bursting with firewood, evening had come, and she suddenly realized that it was getting quite dark. Well, she wasn't lost, she knew how to get home, and the moon made it quite easy to see the way. So she turned with her huge bundle of wood, and started back along the path.

She had not gone far when she heard the cry. It was a howling, like that of wolves, but somehow more frightening. And Marie-Rose remembered that after Mass on Sunday, when the women were gossiping on the church steps, one or them had said that there was a pack of loups-garous in the forest.

Of course, what Marie-Rose should have done then was to drop all the firewood and run, run with all her might, but she had spent such a long time picking it up — it would mean that she had wasted her whole afternoon. The cry sounded quite far away, and she was moving quickly, even with her load of wood. So she continued on her way. But the wood was heavy; she began to slow down. Soon she was walking even more slowly. Much too slowly.

The pack of loups-garous drew near, and it chanced that the last one in the line looked sideways and saw Marie-Rose carrying her burden along the path.

The loup-garou left the pack and began to follow her.

At first Marie-Rose noticed nothing. Then, when she became aware that there was something behind her on the trail, she looked around. A huge animal was pursuing her — an animal with glowing eyes, running sometimes on his hind legs, sometimes on all fours, with its fangs bared and its claws extended — it was a loup-garou!

At that moment Marie-Rose finally did what she should have done much earlier. She let all her kindling drop to the ground. Stumbling over her long shawl, she thrust it back over her shoulders and sped down the path, screaming. Her shawl flew out behind her as she ran.

But the loup-garou ran faster still. He was gaining on her. Soon he was so close that she could hear his footfalls on the path. Then she heard the rasping of his breath. And then the gnashing of his teeth. With that, she knew that in another moment he would fall upon her. And that would be the end of her.

But as she realized all this, she saw ahead of her the edge of the woods, and the back door of her house. She was almost home! With a final burst of speed, a spurt of energy, she hurled herself forward through the trees, pushed open the door, rushed in and slammed it — right in the face of the loup-garou. She was safe, because a loup-garou is a creature of the out-of-doors and will never go into a place where the doors and windows are shut. She leaned back against the door, her heart racing; she could hear her heartbeat so clearly, and at the same time, outside, she could hear the loup-garou as it prowled around the house.

It wouldn't go away.

She had no idea how long she lay against the door, listening. Finally she heard a rustling of the underbrush, and then silence. The loup-garou was gone.

Marie-Rose let out her breath, threw her shawl on a hook, threw herself into bed fully clothed, and fell asleep instantly. She did not even stir when her husband Luc returned, early in the morning, and crept into bed beside her.

When she awakened and found herself still in her clothes, she remembered the events of the previous night. Well, she was home, and she was safe.

She would go back later that morning and pick up the kindling. Luckily there were some bits of wood left in the kindling box, just enough for a fire in the stove. Marie-Rose heated water for *une bouillie*, a porridge, while Luc got up and dressed. They sat down to breakfast in silence, but when Luc put the spoon to his mouth, he made a face.

"What's the matter?" asked Marie-Rose.

"I don't know. There's something stuck between my teeth."

"Let me take a look." So Luc opened his mouth and Marie-Rose looked in. Sure enough, there was something stuck between his teeth! She took hold and yanked it out.

What she was holding was two strands of wool. One was red, the other yellow.

She left the room. She went straight to where her shawl was hanging and lifted it off the hook. She spread it out. Yes, there was a fresh tear in the shawl. And the two strands of wool fitted exactly.

Well, she stood there for a long time holding the truth in her hands, and she didn't know what to do with it.

Finally she picked up the shawl and went back to Luc, who was finishing his breakfast. "Luc, I have something to show you." She held up the shawl with its broken threads, and the two strands of wool. "Look!"

And he looked at the torn shawl, at the wool she had drawn from his mouth, and he said, "That's right, it was me. I'm a loup-garou."

And Marie-Rose, she began to cry.

Luc said, "Ah, Marie-Rose, don't cry! Can you deliver me?"

"Deliver you, what do you mean?"

"If you can wound me while I am running loup-garou, wound me and draw blood — a drop of blood is enough — then I will take human shape, immediately. Then, I must go to a priest and confess my sins. If he forgives me in the name of God, I will never run loup-garou again. I will be delivered. Can you do this for me?"

"Will it be dangerous?"

"Yes, very dangerous. Will you do it anyway?"

Marie-Rose was silent for a moment. "I'll do my best," she said finally.

That very morning, Luc went to the village blacksmith. "Make me a rake, just the metal part. Make it as wide as my forehead."

The blacksmith measured Luc, and when the rake was ready Luc paid him. He took the rake home and made a short handle out of wood. He made it himself, and he attached it to the rake the blacksmith had made. Then Luc gave it to Marie-Rose and said, "Here is your weapon. Tonight, I must go into the forest again to run loup-garou. I run in a pack, Marie-Rose, and there are ten of us, and we run in single file.

I'm tenth, the last in line. I am going to ask the leader of our pack to run through the forest close to this house, to run into our garden, to pass in front of the big bush at the back, and then run back into the forest again. He will do that, and they will all follow, all in line, every one of them.

"Marie-Rose, you must take your weapon, and go hide behind that bush tonight. You must wait for the loups-garous to come. When they enter the garden, one by one, you must count them. Remember, I'm the tenth. When the tenth loup-garou passes in front of the bush where you are hiding, then — and only then — come out of your hiding place and strike me as hard as you can. Don't miss me when you strike, for if you miss me, Marie-Rose, I won't miss you."

And Marie-Rose realized that, indeed, it would be dangerous.

But that night, there she was, hiding behind the bush, the rake clenched in her hand. She heard the howling of the loups-garous getting louder and louder as they approached. And then the leader came bounding into the garden, a hideous animal. Marie-Rose thought that she would die of fright, but she grasped her weapon and held still. The loup-garou came up to the bush, turned and ran back into the forest. One. Another loup-garou followed. Two. Then three, four, five. Marie-Rose raised her weapon slightly. Six. Seven, eight, nine — she waited. She waited.

Nine. Ah, no! She must have counted wrong! But no, there he was, the tenth loup-garou, the last! He had slowed down so that all the rest would be gone when he came. As he rushed towards the bush, Marie-Rose came out, raised her weapon and struck.

But even before the creature fell to the ground, it was no longer a loup-garou. It was Luc her husband, and now he lay with stripes of blood flowing from his forehead.

"Luc, are you delivered? Did I do it properly?"

"Ah, yes, Marie-Rose," breathed Luc, "you have delivered me. Help me up, and lead me to the priest."

So Marie-Rose helped Luc to his feet. And they both went to see the priest. And Luc confessed his sins, and the priest forgave him in the name of God, and after that Luc never again ran loup-garou.

Ozzie Hardin and the Feu Follet
Steve Luxton

"This story was told to me over a beer by Ozzie Hardin.
A canny customer, Ozzie was a woodsman who lived in
Waterville, a small village down in Quebec's Eastern
Townships. A woodsman? That's an understatement if
ever there was one! He was such a good trapper, wild
honey gatherer, forest mushroom hunter, et cetera,
that some of the locals, who were and still are a pretty
superstitious lot, used to whisper the old guy had
otherworldly connections. This was silliness, since
there was one thing Ozzie wasn't — even if he only had
a grade six education — andthat was superstitious. He
always used his head, rarely lost it, and was, I can assure
you, as practical as a deer rifle safety-catch. Which
attitude was the secret of his success as a fisher — and
this brings me to the story he told me at the village
hotel of how he met the feu follet."

Ozzie Hardin was a trout fisher *par excellence*. No one could
outcatch him. He was, however, not like other country
anglers — he didn't hoard his secrets. Everyone knew where
he pulled out his gleaming, deep-bellied trout. They just

didn't dare go there anyhow. I'm talking about that memorable waste stretch outside Waterville which the locals call the "burnt place" — the Brûlé.

The Brûlé is a spruce bog three miles out of town.

There's a dirt road that shies around it, nicking one corner. Step off its gravel and you find yourself standing on a square mile of sucking, quaking jello, surrounded by oily puddles and corpse-plants. The Brûlé is also called the "Place of the Feu Follet." Feux follets are eerie things: flaming swamp gas — or foxfire. Back in the Brûlé, behind a line of bristly spruces, there's a trout-filled pond where the feux follets throng.

Old Ozzie Hardin just chuckled at the superstitions surrounding the spot and fished there anyhow. Let other men shake — that was his line. That is, it was till one evening ten years ago when the drop of darkness caught him in there! That almost spooked him, he later muttered to me in the Manor de Waterville — the night coming on so sudden like that, and the greasy vapours smoking off the peat hummocks.

If you're the trembly kind, this place of flaring swamp gas isn't for you, with its bellowing frogs, dirty sucking noises, and thrashing night-beasts arrowing through the Labrador Tea. To Ozzie Hardin, these sounds were just the swamp wishing him a friendly good night. It took more than them to get the wind up in him.

The bog obliged. Out of nowhere, a ball of sick blue-green light drifted up from a mound and paused in mid-air as if looking at him. Ozzie started taking down and packing his fishing rod. Not that he was scared, mind you.

Then, on the other side of him — to the left — another fiery gas globe rose. Attending carefully to his things, Ozzie congratulated himself he wasn't skittish like some other men he knew. He headed for the windrow of spruce separating the pond from the rest of the bog. Once past the trees, then no problem ... Not that there *were* any problems.

Without warning, down the dry path before him, a big moonlit pond appeared that had never been there before. It wavered, then tilted. Next it climbed up on its end and came boiling right at the old fisher. That feu follet was so big and bright, Ozzie told me, he just about stopped dead in his tracks, waiting further instructions from Hell!

The superstitious ones in that region have a story about the feux follets, you see. According to them, the feux follets are sinners so evil even Hell can't hold them. Sort of like the six Lennoxville bikers who got killed by their own chapter of the Hell's Angels because they were too wild. So the devil, sick and tired, exiles these demons to a place even worse than Hell — a Canadian spruce bog! Of course, given the opportunity, once they're there, they raise even more Hell ...

No matter how hard Ozzie Hardin blinked, that giant feu follet weltered in front of him. By this time, Ozzie Hardin was a believer — the more so because he could see what the demon was about. On either side of the narrow path where he stood, the bog was inky and bottomless. That foxfire was trying to blind and then drown him!

Ozzie took measures. He began tossing away everything on his person that was heavy: his tacklebox — sploosh; his canistered rod — sploosh; his wool mackinaw coat — sploosh; he even extracted his fold-up knife ...

The knife!

Then Ozzie remembered the rest of the story, the bit that talked about the only known antidote. First, you had to have a needle. In full view of the fireball, you shoved the needle into a bit of wood. From that moment, by virtue of the powers in Heaven, the feu follet was constrained to attempt to squeeze through the needle's eye. There are stories like this in the Bible. If you don't remember, it's time you read the Good Book again!

Ozzie had no needle. He had plenty of common sense, however, and the fold-up knife. He pulled out the blade of the knife wide and jammed it in a spruce bar in full view of the feu follet. Then he closed the knife back almost shut, mumblety-peg style, so there was a narrow space between the handle and the blade.

Would the ploy work? Ozzie wondered. At first the feu follet just stood off watching. Then it zigged a bit; then, like a being twice-possessed, it darted forward and lunged again and again at the thread of light between blade and handle.

Whew!

Ozzie knew he couldn't stick around to goggle, though. Once that thing succeeded in wriggling through, it could get back on its former track! The old fisher rushed past the tangled feu follet, through the prickly fence of spruce, and over a country mile of quaking peat and corpse plants to the dirt road.

He slumped down against a log. He wasn't a young man, Ozzie Hardin.

What a silly dream he'd had!

In a few minutes he'd got his breath back and he started thinking of home. He eased himself up.

As he stepped back onto the gravel, he glanced over his shoulder at the dark bog. Maybe his eyes were deceiving him, but they'd caught a small light way in there — a turquoise bead that, as it rose, began to swirl like a pitcher's arm gaining power, and grow red, like something in a rage.

Could it be the freed feu follet?

But before Ozzie Hardin could answer his own question, it was coming at him *fast* — so fast that he felt just like some

World War II soldier watching the tracer bullet that was to kill him come whooshing down through the air.

The fisher stood there paralyzed, stiffer than a perch pulled out of a lake in January and laid out on the ice! Then, somehow, at the last moment, he came to his senses and moved. He twisted left, half ducking. And it was a good job he did, because there was an airy shriek and inches from his ear, a deadly *"Thunk!"*

Ozzie's eyes slid right. A cloud of blue smoke steamed, and in the middle of it his fold-up knife still quivered, jammed in a trunk.

The feu follet, freeing itself, had ridden it in! Gleaming over the dark fields, the feu follet arced back towards the heart of The Brûlé …

It was a near-do for the old man all right. After he told me his story, the old fisher slid his prize knife across the table. He didn't need it anymore, he said — too old to go fishing, even for the fat trout out in The Brûlé.

I still have that knife. I keep it in my glove compartment, just in case.

The Lady in the Snow

J. Antonin Friolet

"I come from a middle-class family and I have always
enjoyed a good life, sheltered in good measure from
those periodical onslaughts that assail one's world. Oh,
there were cloudy moments that reminded me to be
thankful for the sunshine that was abundant; tears are
as good for the soul as is the rain for the soil. My father
was a contractor-builder who gave us amply what we
needed. My mother imparted to me a few gems of her
wisdom which influenced my judgement of others and
truly shaped my life: 'Never forget that you are inferior
to no one, superior to no one, but equal to everyone.'
That probably made me a cynic — I have deep empathy
for the wretched one, great admiration for the humble
one, and deep abhorrence for the inflated ego. Mother
had also counselled: 'Always aim for two things in life: a
good living, and Heaven.' I have always managed to
make a good living but, as for Heaven, I suspect there
are many who would prefer that I go somewhere else.
They might get their wish yet. I taught school for a
while, joined the Royal Canadian Air Force in 1940 to be
a pilot, but later transferred to Public Relations, where I
met some of the notables of the world; went to McGill

University for one year with a view to becoming a lawyer; left when our first-born was stricken with cerebral palsy; freelanced in advertising in Montreal prior to returning to New Brunswick, where the taxpayers paid me a handsome wage until my retirement seven years ago. My first wife was a rare gem. We produced three daughters; two are still living and doing me proud. Widowed in 1976, I remarried five years later to an equally wonderful lady from Toulouse.

My ancestor, a French Huguenot, came from Provence, near the enchanting Riviera. I have distant cousins in Switzerland and on the Côte d'Azur, whom we visit every other year. Life, with all its comforts and blessings, is wonderful."

▼▼▼

It was the night of March 28 in 1907, and cold and bitter it was on the North Shore. The winds whistled and howled in the darkness as the snow swept over the plains of Pokesuedie. For a week now it had been unbearably cold, but the winds had been subdued until that afternoon when, with no warning, strong gusts swept the snow from the northwest and right across the exposed island. It piled deep on the road and around a little shack of a house set in a desolate clearing on that island, hardly half a mile from the wooden bridge that connects the island to the mainland of Lower Caraquet.

As if the winds and snow were not enough, the mercury had dropped far below zero and the little house was fast being surrounded by a heavy cloak of hard white snow. The blizzard would hold its breath for one brief moment, then it would hiss with the power and fury of a hurricane. At every gust the house shook and twisted and almost lifted from its foundation. The roof creaked, and the tar paper fluttered in the wind and tore off, revealing open cracks in the construction, and the chimney pipe rattled and tugged at its haywire moorings.

Inside, in a corner near a stove that had given out its last spark hours ago, a mother and her two children lay huddled on the cold bare floor. A stub of a candle flickered as the wind seeped through chinks in the walls and broken windows. There was no furniture. The snowstorm had outlasted the supply of firewood, and the stove had claimed the mother's rocking chair, the homemade table, and every piece of furniture that could be broken up. The food, too, was all gone, except for some frozen vegetables that could not be thawed and cooked for want of firewood. Even the drinking water, in the pail hanging by a nail on the wall, had frozen into a solid mass.

Hugging her two children — one was a nineteen-month-old baby girl and the other a four-year-old boy — so that her closeness would give them warmth, Christine, the mother, waited. The wind hissed in the night and the windows rattled and the candle burnt itself out slowly. Cold, hunger and thirst were added to a throbbing misery that ruled her whole body and tortured her brain. Migraine, they call it nowadays. Christine waited and hoped and prayed that her husband would return soon.

He had gone out early in the afternoon to get some wood and some food from their nearest neighbour. He had bundled up his third child, a forty-day-old boy, and strapped him onto a small sled. Why he had taken the baby, the youngest of his children, will never be known. He had intended to reach the neighbours, but the blinding snow storm had thrown him off his way and he landed at a house further away, where he left the baby. A while later he ventured out again, groped his way along the Pokesuedie Bridge and landed at the first house on the mainland. What was detaining him? Christine wondered. The children, now too weak and spent to cry with abandon, moaned through chattering teeth. And Christine, too, sobbed in silence, forsaken, her misery unknown to neighbours enjoying the warmth of their homes.

Hours — eternities — passed, and the husband did not return. Christine, her feet cold and her fingers numb, could bear it no longer. Her whole body aching, she got to her feet, wrapped her baby in a heavy red patchwork blanket and the boy in whatever clothes she could find and she opened the door into the night. The candle went out and there was total darkness. The wind literally swept Christine off her feet and the cold air hit her face like the blade of a sword.

Yet she convinced herself that she must go on. For the sake of her two children, she steeled her courage. Bracing herself against the strong icy winds, with her boy clutching her flimsy coat, she moved painfully forward, stumbling backward when the winds pushed harder in her face and stifled her, but always holding the infant to her bosom. The hunger, thirst, and cold she had endured in the last hours had demanded too much of her energy and strength; now winds like icy fingers fastened around her delicate throat and impaired her breathing. She knew she could never make it to the neighbour's house; in fact, she knew now that she had gone the wrong way in the darkness. She was doomed. Her hands and feet were now like dead weights, and her skin was raw and freezing. The northwest blizzard lashed at her face and through her thin garments. She stumbled and fell, never to get up. With a little moan, she huddled against a picket fence, covered herself as best she could with the blanket and held close to her children, waiting.

At the house where Christine's husband had gone, the kitchen stove was shooting sparks from its open front grate and throwing out a warm heat. The evening meal had been substantial and Christine's husband had had his fill. Once the table was cleared, the grown-ups settled at the table for a few games of forty-five, a popular card game in winter months. It is said that the husband showed no sign of concern for his wife and the two children he had left at home. When the time came to go to bed he made a feeble attempt to go home, but it took little persuasion to make him spend the night in warmer surroundings. When asked about his wife and children, he shrugged and mumbled: "Christine n'a pas peur de rien. Inquiétez-vous pas!" *Christine fears nothing. Don't you worry!*

Time passed and Christine's mind became confused. Four months before she had been living at South Nelson, near Newcastle, where her husband had worked as a woodsman. Because of the hardships there, they had decided to return to her parents' home in Pokesuedie. They had left a daughter, Elizabeth, with an aunt at Lagaceville. Now, the young mother was thankful to God that one, at least, was being spared.

If only they had all stayed at South Nelson, Christine thought. Her headache passed and she was not hungry anymore; a feeling of blessed peace came over her. Before her eyes were the nicest patterns she had ever seen, beautiful brainwaves fighting among themselves for a part in her subconscious. In this kaleidoscopic arrangement of shapes and colours, her mind sank back and wandered away. The clock of time pushed back: back to the days upon which she had given birth to each of her four children; further back to her wedding day; further back to her carefree youth when, standing at the beach and facing the rain and winds, she had looked like a weathercock, her thin cotton dress pressed against her limbs and her long hair flowing in the strong breeze; back further to those happy moments on sunny afternoons when she swam in the nude with other children; back to the innocence of her childhood, when life had no meaning yet and things did not matter too much; and finally, back to the warmth of her mother's bosom where, as an infant, she had learned a few prayers. How did that prayer go now? "O Lord, I am heartily sorry for having offended Thee ..." and then she could think no more. There were no nightmares to haunt her last moments. Christine had no cause or reason for remorse. She had been a good child, a good daughter, a good wife, a good mother.

Now the beautiful colours were more animated than before, playing foolishly behind her eyelids, gathering in a round ball that exploded and shattered her brain. Complete unconsciousness. The icy fingers of death crept along her legs and arms, found their way into her breasts, crushing her heart and lungs and stifling all life. Hours passed. The winds blew and hissed and piled more snow in drifts and mounds over Pokesuedie Island, until there was nothing but a tattered bit of red cloth sticking out of the snow near a fence. The cloth fluttered in the wind like the feathers of a dead bird, just a few yards away from Christine's neighbour's house.

Morning came and Nature stood still. Mounds of crisp white snow shone like tinsel in the bright sun. The tattered cloth fluttered no more; it lay limp and ominous. When Christine's husband came home, trying to think up a good excuse for his delay, he saw the red rag but he did not stop. But when he saw the door of his house wide open and half-filled with snow, he knew then that tragedy had struck. The alarm was raised and finally the red rag was spotted. Christine was dead, frozen stiff, and the little boy, hunched next to his mother, was frozen too. Only the baby slept peacefully, in the blanket in which her mother had wrapped her.

Anna, the baby girl of the tragedy, survived this dreadful ordeal with frostbitten feet. She was cared for by relatives in Pokesuedie and friends of her family in Lower Caraquet. In 1920, at age fourteen, she married Edmond Morais of Cara-quet, an industrious young man who managed to make a living in the hard depression years that followed the First World War. But he died in 1937, when Anna was only thirty-one — a beautiful, blond, blue-eyed woman. Now she was a widow, with a family of eight, and she relied very much on her eldest son, Albert, then sixteen, to manage through those difficult years. Albert became a highly regarded school building inspector with the Department of Education. Another son, Lorenzo, became a very successful businessman, as well as mayor of Caraquet and a member of the New Brunswick Legislature. By all accounts, he was Caraquet's first millionaire. He established La Place Caraquet, a commercial centre in the heart of Caraquet which is an eloquent monument to his grandmother Christine, and to his own mother, Anna, who survived this awful ordeal in 1907 and is still alive today.

▼▼▼▼▼▼

Maggie Lochlin's Last Storm
Teresa Doyle

"This story was told to me by Lorne Johnston in 1988.
Lorne's father ran the cannery at Clear Spring, Prince
Edward Island when Lorne was a teenager. Lorne led a
long and colourful life. He was a lobster fisher, a
rumrunner and a sailor. But most of all he was a
storyteller. When Lorne told a story you could smell the
salt air, you could feel the chill of a cold April morning,
you could see the black of the water against the white
of an iceberg. Sadly, I heard too few of his stories
before he died in 1990."

▼▼▼

Maggie smoked the pipe. I remember her down at the
canteen in the fish cannery. Oh, I guess that would be in the
'20s. I was just a teenager. My father had just bought the
cannery and we'd moved up to Clear Spring. You know, up
past Goose River on the north side of the Island. The
Northsiders, they're a clannish bunch — Scotch Catholics
— but they always treated us well.

Maggie was married to a Hughie Gillis. "Hughie Lochlin"
they called him. He'd been dead for years. The old lady, she
was lonely I guess. Anyway, you'd see her coming, walking

down through the fields to the cookhouse and then on over to the canteen, where she'd be talking to the fishers.

The men would crowd around her and put the questions to her. Would tomorrow be a good day to set the traps? Is the weather about to turn? Will it be fit to sail in the morning?

Maggie had the gift, you see. Had it since she was twelve. Her grandfather was the one that brought it with him from the Old Country. He never forgot it and when Maggie was still a child, just before the great storm, just before the Yankee Gale, he taught her how to do it. That was 1873. Twelve hundred Yankee schooners went down. Cattle drowned in the fields. A storm sure the likes no one had ever seen before. Well, the Northsiders fared better than the Yanks. Sure, they couldn't afford a schooner to fish in. No, folks around here were still fishing in the dories. And the men in Clear Spring, well their feet never left the dry land that day. The old fellow seen it coming and they knew better than to question what he'd seen.

It was MacGillivary who took me up there, Billy Mac-Gillivary. He knew Maggie Lochlin pretty well. He sort of took care of her, you see. MacGillivary was a bit of a queer stick himself. If Maggie was wantin' for anything he'd sorta get the call, ye see. He'd be out splitting wood or something, and he'd just get this feeling and he'd know he'd have to go into Bear River and pick her up some things. It wasn't ever much. All she got was tea and tobacco. Funny how old folk get. There's not too much they really want to eat. Anyway, he always knew when she needed something. No one would ever have to tell him. He'd just hear her voice in his head and then he'd go on in to Bear River. He always knew to buy her tobacco at Joe Larry MacDonald's store. The other store was owned by a Bill MacDonald — terrible Conservatives they were, and God, she hated the

Tories. She'd never let on, though. She'd just say their tobacco was stale.

Anyway, MacGillivary had some things for her this one day and he was heading up there after supper. A few of the lads said they'd take a walk up with him and I just tagged along.

I knew a bit what to expect. My mother often went up to visit the old lady, bring her a bottle of jam, make sure she was okay, and sometimes the old lady would read for her. You know, them times lots of people could read your cup. You know, tea leaves. But this was different. Nobody could see into the future like Maggie Lochlin.

We got there just after dark. The old lady beckoned us in and put on the kettle. Johnny Angus was there and he was awful nervous — the priest wasn't too fond of this business and Johnny Angus lived in fear of the Church. Maggie, she made a cup of tea and we all sat around swapping yarns.

After a bit, Maggie went to the loom and got a short piece of spun wool. She went to the cupboard and brought down a strange tin dish. I'd never seen anything quite like it. It was two-tiered and round. Maggie spun one end of the yarn into a tiny ball. She set the ball on the top part of the tin dish and let the end of the yarn trail down to the bottom part. Then she grabbed a set of tongs and went to the fire and fetched a coal. She put the coal on the dish where it could smoulder the trailing yarn. Then she turned the kerosene lamp down, and we were silent.

Within minutes the smouldering yarn gave forth a curl of smoke. Maggie's eyes fixed on this smoke and not a muscle did she move as she sat and watched. The lads around the table were afraid to breathe.

Finally, the smoke died away and Maggie slowly pulled her thoughts to the present.

"There's goin' to be a grandaddy of a storm," she says. "A storm to rival the Saxby Gale of '96 or the great Yankee Gale. But I won't be here to see it. I can't bear to see any more hardship and heartbreak. It's more than my soul can bear. No, I won't live to see it. It'll come just at the full moon in October. The boats will all be on blocks for the winter. No, no one will drown — not if you listen to what I'm telling you. The cookhouse will go and the cannery too. There won't be a wharf left from St. Peters to Naufrage ... but, I don't understand ... I see the boats from Clear Spring all piled up at the bridge."

At this point Johnny Angus cut in. "But Ma'am, the bridge is a good mile inland and there's nothing but a bit of a brook running out to the sea! Surely this time you've made a mistake."

"I know what I saw and there'll be no mistake about it. Now if you don't mind I'd like to get to bed."

We didn't know what to make of Maggie's words. No one wanted to doubt the old lady, but how in Christ could a dozen lobster boats end up a mile from the shore? Well, she was getting up in years. Maybe she'd finally lost the gift.

That was late August. Within a couple of weeks Maggie decided she'd go down to visit her daughter in Boston. She kept talkin' about the great storm and how she didn't want to see it. Well, she never did. She wasn't in Boston a week before she passed away.

People got nervous then. I think that's why we fared better in Clear Spring. Come October, folks moved their gear well away from the shore and tied things down good and solid.

The storm hit with no warning at all. Even the old people said they'd never seen worse. The breakers were seven fathom, and it being the full moon, the tide was at its highest.

At Naufrage the beach was swept clean. Everything went into the harbour — every building and boat. Lobster canneries, dories, cookhouses, traps, ropes were swept away all along the north side. Everywhere, that is, except Clear Spring.

Clear Spring is just a tiny brook with a wide mouth down at the shore. That's where the men had their boats up on pilings for the winter. The hurricane-force winds blew hard on the shore and the crashing surf plucked the lobster boats from their moorings and pushed them inland on the flooded brook. The Northsiders couldn't believe their eyes. The boats came to a crashing halt when they struck the bridge, fully one mile from the shore. When the seas calmed again, no one could imagine how those boats had been carried on that tiny brook.

Those of us who had been at Maggie Lochlin's house that night in August had plenty to think about. More than one of us felt bad that we'd doubted the old lady's word.

That was October 1923, and I was eighteen at the time. Well, I've seen a lot of queer sights since then, but I'll never forget Maggie Lochlin's last storm.

▼▼▼▼▼▼

The Ghost Ship

Jocelyn Bérubé
(translated by Shawna Watson)

"I began my storytelling career in 1971, collecting
legends, fairytales and music from the oral tradition.
Over time, I began to write my own stories while
continuing to tell traditional tales. Several versions of
The Ghost Ship are told in the Gaspé region as well
as in Acadia. I hope that this version I have adapted
still has relevance to people today."

▼▼▼

In the old days in France, people felt that the earth around
them was shrinking. They dreamed of voyages that would open
the horizon. They hoped that, by travelling, the world might
grow bigger again. And so it was that François de Nerac, the
eldest son of a peasant family, set sail for New France, where
there was plenty of land for anyone willing to travel so far.

François left behind his fiancée, Blanche. When he bid her
farewell he held her close and promised that as soon as a house
was built, she would come to join him. And then they kissed and
said good-bye.

As his ship reached the New World and sailed up the Saint
Lawrence River, François was overwhelmed by the expanse of

sparsely populated land. In his first letter to Blanche he wrote:

"Ici, les forêts sont immenses comme l'océan que j'ai traversé ... Here, the forests are as vast as the ocean I have crossed ..."

Soon, François set to work clearing his land and building his house. When he was lonely, he thought of Blanche. He imagined her singing and telling stories to their future children in the evening when the work was done. Finally, the house was finished and François stood back and admired his work. "One day this cabin of pine needles will be a castle made of stone as sturdy as nearby Cap Diamant!" he promised himself.

That night, by candlelight, François sat at his pine table and wrote to Blanche that all was ready:

"Come join me Blanche, my destiny, my wild rose. Together with our children we will discover this fairy-tale country where freedom is a treasure I have been given ..."

As soon as Blanche received this letter, she prepared to leave for New France. Along with many other women, she boarded the next sailing ship headed there.

The women sailed for many long winter months of misery on the often turbulent sea. Sometimes, on clear nights, they gathered on the deck and sang love songs. The captain didn't mind — he said it helped the crew to sleep.

"In the deep of the night, you are my shining light.

In the deep of the night, you are my guiding light."

The sweet singing caused Blanche to think of the coming spring, when she would see François. She pictured his face lit with a smile, his shining dark eyes. She dreamed of the children they would have, the laughter they would share. She looked up at the spectacular night sky and silently asked the stars if they, like tea leaves in the bottom of a cup, spelled out her destiny.

One dark night the ship reached the Gulf of Saint Lawrence, but the women did not come forth to sing, nor did Blanche gaze up at the stars. Not one star shone down on them this night. The sky was a mass of swirling clouds, the wind was fierce and the ship rocked. Waves washed the deck and the women huddled together in the cabins. They could tell that this was to be the worst storm yet.

Soon the clouds broke and torrents of rain flooded down on the raging sea. "Avast! Lower the outer jib," the captain called to his men. "Trim the topsails! Look alive there!"

Wind filled the sails and the ship raced through the night. It was then that the vessel was spied by a pirate ship drifting with the current. The darkness was thick enough to cut with a knife, but the white flags identifying the French ship could still be seen. The pirates acted quickly and fired their cannons in a direct assault.

The French had no idea what had hit them. Then the dark figures of dozens of men swung onto their bridge. There was a bloody battle, and all of the French crew were killed. The pirates did not kill the women, however; they rounded them up and took them as prisoners onto their own ship. Once aboard the pirate ship, Blanche struggled to look back at the French ship. She saw it sink into the black and raging depths of the Saint Lawrence.

The women were thrown into the hold and heavily guarded by several pirates. They were visited only once by the pirate captain, who looked each woman over with a cunning eye. One of them was to become his bride.

At last the storm ended and, by morning, the captain had made his choice of the women. Blanche was to marry him. The heartbroken prisoners were assembled on the bridge to witness the event.

It was a windy but sun-filled morning. Blanche stood on the deck looking out at the icy waters and listening to the cries of the gulls. She appeared very calm, as if resigned to her fate. Then all of a sudden, despite the captain's watchful eye, she picked up her skirts, ran across the deck to the bow of the ship and threw herself into the freezing waters. Instantly, all of the other women ran forward, gave a great cry and leapt to join Blanche under the waves.

The captain stared, dumbfounded. Then, in a fury to possess Blanche, he, too, ran to the edge and dove into the water to retrieve her. Before the dismayed eyes of his crew, the captain froze to death.

All was quiet on the ship as the men stared into the water, and for a moment the vessel appeared to glide aimlessly. But then a huge shadow darkened the waters, and when the pirates raised their heads they saw an enormous rock looming ahead. And there, on top of the jagged rock, was the ghostly figure of Blanche in her long bride's veils, glaring down at them. The pirates were frozen beneath her stare and the ship swiftly crashed against the rock and shattered into a hundred pieces.

In the spring François discovered that the French ship would never come to port. His bride, his destiny, was still out there somewhere, under the waves.

Since that time, Blanche's jagged rock has been known as Rocher Percée, or Pierced Rock. It is said that sometimes, at dusk, fishers still catch glimpses of the women who were killed on that fateful voyage. Like sirens, the women return alone to the rocky coast, but when they see the fishers they quickly flee into the twilight, leaving only the echo of a song.

"In the deep of the night ..."

Fishers say that the pirate ship has become a Ghost Ship. They claim that on foggy nights it can still be seen in the Gulf of Saint Lawrence, sailing without captain or masts, searching for the port it will never find, the harbour that will never bid it welcome.

No-Post

Nan Gregory

"I make my living as a storyteller. I think that's special. But there's nothing special about me, nothing exceptional about my background. Sometimes when I read that another teller 'has come from a long line of storytellers,' I feel self-conscious, as if I had less right to be a teller than they, because my mother was a housewife and my father was a lawyer, and I know next to nothing about my grandparents. When I was little my mother read to me and my father told me Bible stories. I remember those times fondly, but I don't think I tell stories because of that. I think I tell stories because stories are an expression of something natural and human. I think every child was born to love the order and the meaning that are Story's best gift to the world.

If you have a feeling for telling stories, go right ahead, jump in. No one has a better right than you to tell a story that you love. If you wish to tell my story, you are most welcome. Use it as a springboard and make it your own. And if you have a spare moment, drop me a line and tell me how it went."

I t was after midnight. The little orange numbers on the dash said 12:55, and it was pouring rain. I was hours from my motel room, miles from my bed. I was on the road, driving through the dark, heading for Tofino. I was on holiday. I was going to spend a weekend at the beach — a few days in a place where nobody knew me and nobody would ask me to do anything for them.

I'd had a rough start. Early on I'd missed my ferry. Then I'd had a flat tire. Shortly after that, I'd nearly hit a deer. Now I was driving down the hill outside Port Alberni, sucking on a large cup of bitter, black corner store coffee, trying to stay awake, peering through the rain-washed windshield into the thick night. I drove slowly, trying to see, thinking it was like devils were dancing on the roof of the car pouring buckets of water onto the windshield, because no matter how fast the wipers went they couldn't keep the windshield clear.

At the bottom of the hill the road curves sharply, and just beyond the curve is a bridge. The locals call it the Sproat Lake Bridge. It's not a big bridge. It doesn't have trusses or anything over the top. It's really only an overpass crossing a bit of a river, and leading up to it are those sloping cement barriers called no-posts.

As I say, I was driving slowly because I was having such trouble seeing, and when I came around the corner I could just make out someone standing by the no-post, hitchhiking. When I got a little closer I saw that the hitchhiker was a girl. She wasn't wearing a hat or a coat. She wasn't wearing boots or carrying an umbrella. She had on a little sleeveless party dress — a mini dress — and high-heeled shoes. Her hair was long and dark, and hung below her shoulders, thick with rain.

I stopped the car and opened the door. The two of us moved my books and my briefcase off the passenger seat into the back and she got in. I gave her a sweater to wrap around her shoulders. "Thanks," she said, "I'm awful wet." She told me that she had been to a dance in Port Alberni, and that her boyfriend had got drunk at the dance, and after the dance he had driven down the hill, weaving so wildly from one side of the road to the other that when they got to the Sproat Lake Bridge she'd told him to let her out before he killed them both. That was why I'd found her, hitchhiking, in the middle of the rainstorm, in the middle of the night. She told me she lived at the reserve at Long Beach, and I said, "That's lucky, I'm going right past there. I'll take you home."

We drove for a couple of hours without talking very much, and then we came to where the road straightens out along the beach, and you can see the breakers shining, even at night, and the houses of the reserve nestled in amongst the trees. One of the houses had a light on. The girl said, "That's my house."

I stopped the car by the side of the road and waited for her to get out. She didn't move. "Okay," I said. "You're home. Safe and sound." All of a sudden she began to cry.

"What's the matter?" I asked.

She told me she'd had an awful fight with her dad earlier that night. He didn't like her boyfriend. He said her boyfriend was too old for her. He said he was a trouble-maker. He said he was a drunk. He refused to let her got to the dance. She'd told her dad he could go to hell for all she cared. She'd slammed the door in his face. She said her boyfriend had gunned the car out of the driveway so hard the gravel sprayed up high behind the back wheels, and in the rear view mirror she's seen her father watching her from the window. Now she was afraid to go home. She didn't say she was frightened he would beat her. She never said that. But I got the feeling that's what she was thinking.

I told her, "Just sneak in the back way and go to sleep. Things will calm down by morning."

"Oh, no," she said. "He always waits up for me."

"So what do you want to do?" I asked.

She turned to me. "Could you go up there and talk to my dad? Tell him he was right? Say I'm really, really sorry. Could you do that?"

I didn't know what else to do. I got out of the car and walked up the driveway. The rain was easing off. I knocked on the door. It was opened by a very weary looking man.

"Excuse me," I said, "I have your daughter in my car."

He shook his head. The porch light made black pits of his eyes.

"She's very upset," I continued. "She asked me to tell you she's sorry."

He smiled a broken smile.

"Well," I said expectantly, "is it okay? Can she come in?"

He spoke. His voice was like a hollow well. "My daughter's dead," he said. "Died in a car accident five years ago. Skidded into the no-posts at the Sproat Lake Bridge." He stepped back into the shadows of the house and shut the door.

I turned around and ran back to my car. It was empty. The front seat was cluttered with junk again as if I'd never had a passenger at all. I looked back. The house was dark.

I drove to the motel and began to empty my car: suitcase from the back, books, briefcase from the front seat. I picked up the sweater. The wool was damp.

I stood there in the drizzle for a long time, holding the sweater, wondering. Who was it out there hitchhiking, trying so hard to come home?

Bag o' Bones

Louis Bird

"I was born in the wilderness on March 4, 1934, and I
am a native of the First Nation on the southwest coast of
the Hudson Bay Lowland. The first twenty-five years of
my life were spent in the wilderness learning how to
survive by hunting and trapping. Learning survival skills
means knowing and understanding that the environment
contains our ancestors. It means learning to understand
the world in terms of the culture of our ancestors.

It was only in 1957 that I began to learn to work as a
wage earner. I began to learn white man's world and
culture. In 1969 I began to study the English Language.
In 1974 I began to collect the stories that are part of our
cultural tradition. I started with simple stories and later
began to collect legends. It was easy to tell the legends
because I have memorized quite a few. Then I started to
listen to other elders to obtain a variety of versions of the
same legend.

Our Omushkigo (Cree) stories are many, and they
are difficult to translate into English. (Omushkigo is our
tribal name. 'Cree' is a name invented by the French
people in the 1600s.) The stories are also very old. Our
ancestors told these stories before Europeans came into

the Bay area. The legends were used for educational purposes. They opened up subjects for the people to talk about, and also entertained people of all ages.

I haven't yet been able to write down all the legends that I have collected. Once these legends are written down, they will be limited, they won't be as flexible as they should be to be useful. Our legends will be nothing but 'simple folklore' unless we study the oral history first, and understand that these stories are believed to be the history of humankind — and even the pre-history of human beings. The stories are useful in many ways, but what is required is a way to bring them out from those elders who are still living. They have to be convinced that they are the last living history of our people in the land. There is still much work to be done collecting the different kinds of stories in our culture before all our elders pass away.

Bag o' Bones is an old story that has many variations. Coastal Natives often asked Roman Catholic missionaries about their strange experiences with the Skeleton. The missionaries didn't explain, but they did tell our elders that, according to the Old Testament, after Cain murdered his brother, he was condemned to wander the earth as punishment for his crime ... But our people didn't buy this. According to them, the Skeleton has at least two explanations: 1) It is the illusion created by a shaman; 2) It is a taboo, doomed human, a blasphemer who inevitably brings bad luck to whoever sees it, hears it and talks to it."

A long time ago, before the Europeans came in, the people of the James Bay and Hudson Bay area experienced strange things in their life. One of them was what they called "skeletons" or the "Bag o' Bones." This was something that looked like a skeleton and seemed to travel in the atmosphere. It travelled sometimes in the higher atmosphere, sometimes with the clouds, and sometimes on the treetops. And it usually travelled, they say, when it was stormy, like in the fall when there was a gust of wind with the snow. They used to say you'd hear this terrible sound, like someone mourning and crying and chattering, as it travelled with the storm clouds. Sometimes, though more rarely, it could be heard on a clear day with not a cloud in the sky.

The Bag o' Bones was always travelling very fast, and always from the northwest to the southeast. Even when the sky was clear, the people usually didn't see it. They could only hear it, and always three times. And even before they heard it, they experienced fear in their body — they'd get chills down the spine. Then they'd hear the voice from the northwest — very far away at first, then closer, then right over their heads. When that happened, some of the people would pass out from fear. Children, as well as adults with little courage, would be paralyzed. In a few minutes when their fear had diminished, they'd hear it again, coming from the southeast; and then one last time from that direction as it faded away. The people who heard it, and the fewer who saw it, described the Bag o' Bones as a human skeleton with a tongue and a bit of windpipe and lung.

Once there were two young men who were travelling in the coastal regions of James Bay and Hudson Bay, following the trails that people used to use when they visited each other. It was the fall, and the geese had already left, the wind was blowing and the clouds were gathering. A storm was coming. These two young men were travelling close to the treeline and they heard a voice during a gust of wind. They knew what it was. Every young man along the coast had been instructed that if he should hear a voice in the lower atmosphere or in a treetop, he should go and investigate and find out where the voice came from. If he found such a thing as a skeleton stuck on top of a tree, he would have to release it.

The two young men followed the voice and found a skeleton stuck on top of a tree. The Bag o' Bones said, "Let me off the tree!"

One of the men didn't want to go any closer because he was afraid; but the other man said they had to release the Bag o' Bones — it was a moral obligation and they had been instructed to do it. The frightened man stayed behind a little and followed the other man, the courageous one. And the courageous one picked up a stick and tied another stick to it until he could reach the skeleton on the treetop. But before they released it, the frightened man said, "Maybe we could ask the skeleton our fortune." He knew that it was supposed to know the future.

So the first man, the brave one, said to the skeleton, "I want you to tell me my future."

And the skeleton said, "Because you had the courage to come and release me, you shall live to be white-haired. You shall live a very long life."

And the other man asked the skeleton, "What about my future?"

And the Bag o' Bones said, "Because you were so afraid that you didn't want to release me, you will not live to see another winter!"

And so it happened that the one who had been told he'd live a long life and be white-haired, did live long; and the other one didn't live to see another winter. And that is one part of the story about the Bag o' Bones.

Even after the Europeans came to our country, the skeleton was seen and heard. The last such sighting was in 1954, and it happened to my own uncle, about eighty miles west of the village of Winisk. My mother, my brother and I were visited unexpectedly by this uncle on a Sunday afternoon. He had never come to visit us before, and he didn't tell us why he came that day. It was years later that he told us how he had been settling down to rest on the trail, with his little dog, when he'd heard the skeleton — that terrible sound like someone trying to speak and cry at the same time. He had been so frightened that he had set off right away in search of other human beings. That is why he came to see us, and he was alive for many years after that.

The Little Boy in the Tree
Basil Johnston, O. Ont.

"The Ojibway words and names in this story translate as:

Puwaugun — Pipe.

Waubizee-quae — Swan Woman.

Nawautin — Peaceful, calm.

Waematik — Heart of an Oak.

Weendigo — A Giant cannibal who stalked
individuals, camps and villages of the Ojibway,
falling on those guilty of excesses, the
improvident and the imprudent. Perpetually
hungry, Weendigo could never requite his
hunger, no matter how much he ate. The more
he ate, the larger he grew, the greater his
hunger.

Maemaegawaehnse — A little being akin to an elf,
who dwells in the forest. This being bears a
special kinship with children, coming to them to
uplift their spirits should they be despondent, or
conducting them back home should they
wander away into the forest on their own. The
little boy in the tree, I believe, was a
Maemaegawaehnse."

One morning, the waters on the opposite shore of the lake tumbled, tossed and rumbled as if huge rocks were being cast upon them. Waubizee-quae looked up from her work. Her heart stopped. To her horror she saw the dreaded Weendigo, a being taller than seven tall men, making his way directly across the lake, bellowing as he heaved the waters with each step. In terror Waubizee-quae seized her son, Nawautin, and fled into the lodge.

"Eeeeeyoooh! You're hurting my hand," complained Nawautin. "What's wrong, Mother? Who's that coming across the lake? Why'd we run inside?"

There was no time for Waubizee-quae to explain what was happening. Besides, she didn't want to frighten her little son; she didn't want to tell him that the giant surging through the water and roaring "I know where you are! You can't hide from me!" was Weendigo. It was too late to tell Nawautin that Weendigo was a cannibal who fed upon human flesh, blood and bones. It was too late to tell him that this monster taller than seven tall men would eat them alive in the next few moments. So she blurted out, "It's grandfather!"

"Come out!" Weendigo roared.

Although Waubizee-quae was pressing her son to her bosom, Nawautin managed to break free with a sudden twist. He bolted outside.

"Come back! Come back," Waubizee-quae cried out.

But Nawautin was already outside greeting the giant, "Grandfather! Grandfather!"

Weendigo stepped ashore, water dripping from his sides. He stopped and looked down at Nawautin. Never had anyone addressed him as "Grandfather." "Where's your mother?" Weendigo demanded in a thunderous voice.

Nawautin pointed to the lodge.

"Where's your father?" Weendigo roared.

"He's away hunting," Nawautin replied without fear.

"Do you have anything to eat?" the giant blared.

Nawautin ran into the lodge. "Grandfather is hungry," he informed his mother.

All Waubizee-quae had to offer Weendigo was a hindquarter of a deer. This the monster devoured in an instant. Then he lay down to sleep, snoring like a cataract. Mother and son went about their work quietly lest they disturb the giant.

It was already late evening when Puwaugun returned home. As he stepped from his canoe, he threw a deer on shore. At that moment Weendigo awoke. He saw the deer, took hold of it, ripped the flesh apart with his hands and his jaws and wolfed it down, while bones crackled and blood dripped down the sides of his mouth. Directly afterward he lay down again to sleep.

That night, Waubizee-quae urged her husband to kill the giant. But Puwaugun said that it would be quite as useless to try to murder the monster as to run away. The best they could hope was for the monster to go away in his own good time.

But the monster remained with them for some time, seizing for himself whatever game Puwaugun brought home from his hunting expeditions. At times, when he was displeased with the quantity of meat that the hunter brought home, Weendigo would roar and threaten to kill him. On these occasions, only Nawautin could soothe the monster by saying, "Grandfather, don't be angry."

At last, after what seemed like months, the monster told Nawautin, "I'm leaving. Except for you, I would have killed all of you by now. If I stay any longer, I will indeed kill you. I need to eat more than what your father has been bringing to me. I must go." And the monster bellowed as he brought down his huge club upon a rock. Fragments flew in all directions, and one of them struck Waubizee-quae in the temple, killing her instantly.

When Puwaugun came home that evening, he found the Weendigo gone and his son crying at Waubizee-quae's side. Puwaugun guessed at once that Weendigo had killed Waubizee-quae.

After preparing his wife's body, Puwaugun buried her next to the great oak that had been her favourite tree. Then he held vigil for four days by the graveside.

Within a few days Puwaugun had to resume hunting in order to provide for his son and for himself. But because Nawautin was young and small, the hunter had to leave him at home in the care of a lady from the village.

When Puwaugun returned from his hunting trip late in the afternoon, his son cried in his arms, "Dad! Can't I go with you? I don't like that woman. I'm lonely and I have nothing to do. Will you take me with you tomorrow?"

Puwaugun felt sorry for his son. He explained that he often had to walk for miles in the forest before he came upon game. Nawautin would never be able to keep up. It was time, however, for Nawautin to begin practicing marksmanship with bow and arrow, and that would give him something to do.

The next day, with the bow and arrow that his father had made for him, Nawautin shot at squirrels and chipmunks and sparrows for most of the morning. For a while it was fun and even exciting for Nawautin to stalk the little birds and animals, to aim and fire at them. But after a while he grew discouraged from missing the little targets. They always sprang out of the way at the last moment.

From time to time — too frequently, thought Nawautin — his guardian, who was an old lady, called, "Nawautin, where are you?"

"Over here!"

"Don't go any further, now, do you hear?"

"No! I won't!"

Nawautin resumed play, but by now he had grown tired of shooting at targets he could not hit. He found a new sport in firing his arrow into the sky to see how high he could send it, and then watching it fall back to earth. After a while Nawautin wearied even of this. One last time he drew the arrow back to his ear and let fly, then watched it fall into a clump of bushes near the oak tree. He unstrung his bow and hung it by the entrance to the lodge, just as his father had told him to do. Then he went in search of his arrow.

But, how strange it was — Nawautin could not find his arrow in the clump of bushes where he had seen it fall.

It was not until his father asked him how his marksmanship had gone that day that Nawautin made mention of his futile attempts and the loss of his arrow. Puwaugun consoled his son by telling him that marksmanship did not come in a day, or several days. As for the loss of the arrow, Puwaugun was stern. "Hunters do not lose their equipment, they look after their bows and arrows," he told his son.

The next day, even though Nawautin eventually shot a squirrel and was filled with a momentary sense of triumph, he soon grew tired of the sport. Again, before putting away his bow and arrow Nawautin fired one last time. He watched his new arrow come down, directly into the clump of bushes where his other arrow had fallen the previous day.

To his astonishment, this time Nawautin saw a little boy standing by the bushes. The boy caught his arrow just as it fell to the ground and made off with it. He ran directly toward the great oak, and vanished into it.

The instant the strange little boy disappeared into the tree, Nawautin ran after him, shouting "My arrow! My arrow! Give me back my arrow! Give me back my arrow!" Moments later he was standing next to the oak. He walked around it deliberately, looking at it from every angle and sounding it with his knuckle. The tree was solid, firm. And yet, he, Nawautin, had seen the strange little boy enter it.

So far as Nawautin knew, the little boy was somewhere within the tree and would answer were Nawautin, with the faith of a six-year-old, only to speak to him. "Give me back my arrow! Father will be angry with me for losing my arrow. I need it. I have nothing else to play with. I need it. I want it back. I need it so that I can practice to be a hunter. Why have you taken my arrow?" As Nawautin talked, the image of a boy's face appeared on the trunk of the oak, like a reflection in a pool of water. Nawautin continued to talk, but he changed his plea, "Come on out. Come out and play. I have no friend, no one to play with. I'm all alone. Won't you come out and play?"

The little boy in the tree replied, "I'll come out if you promise not to tell your father."

Nawautin promised, and the little boy was transformed from image to reality as he stepped out from the oak. The two boys began to play at once, and they continued to play throughout the afternoon until at last the strange little boy, whose name was Waematik, drew up short during a race. He began to tremble and his voice was harsh: "Someone's coming. Your father. Don't say anything and I'll come back tomorrow." With that, Waematik ran to the oak and faded into it.

Nawautin ran down to the shore to meet his father and to tell him the good news — that he had found the arrow he had lost, and that he had shot a squirrel, but it had escaped. Puwaugun was pleased. He wiped perspiration and dirt from his son's brow. "What were you doing just now?" he inquired.

"Nothing. Just playing ... running," Nawautin panted, still trying to get his breath back.

"It's good to play, son, but you musn't play too hard. You must rest from time to time," said Puwaugun.

The next morning, as soon as his father rounded the point and disappeared, Nawautin ran to the oak. "He's gone. You can come out now," he said. Waematik emerged.

All morning the two boys ran races and wrestled, until both were quite exhausted. Every now and then Nawautin had to return his guardian's call: "Nawautin, where are you? Are you all right?"

"Yes! I'm all right."

"Now, don't go too far away."

"I won't. Don't worry."

These calls from Nawautin's guardian frightened Waematik. Each time the guardian called, he wanted to leave at once and Nawautin had to beg his friend to stay and to assure him not to worry — the guardian was old and feeble and short of sight.

After a short rest, the two boys returned to play. Waematik led Nawautin into the forest and taught him how to stalk and shoot rabbits and partridges. By following his friend's directions, Nawautin killed a rabbit. Waematik even knew how to strike a fire and prepare and cook rabbit, although he would not eat.

The moment that Nawautin had finished his meat, he pulled his friend to his feet to resume play. They played hide-and-seek and wrestling, and guessed the names of birds who sang in the forest, gathered plants, climbed trees and imitated raccoons — all new games that Waematik invented.

As soon as Nawautin tired of one, Waematik would invent another. That his friend knew so much more than he, and was stronger and quicker, bothered Nawautin not at all. He was too young and too happy to take notice of these matters.

But for all the delight that Nawautin derived from the many different games, he liked best to pit his strength against Waematik in wrestling. They both groaned in effort and laughed in triumph as they fell to the ground.

Late in the afternoon, Nawautin had just thrown Waematik to the ground when his friend stiffened and his eyes glazed in fright. Waematik stammered, "Someone's coming! Your father! Don't say anything, do you understand?"

As soon as he regained his feet, Waematik fled and disappeared into the mass of the oak. Nawautin stood transfixed, wishing that he too could enter a tree. Then he ran to the shore to await his father.

"Who was here?" Puwaugun asked, even before he stepped from his canoe.

"No one! Why?" Nawautin asked in feigned surprise.

"Because I heard voices long before I came around the point," Puwaugun explained.

"It was I you must have heard. I was shouting and yelling at some crows and ravens who were at the food rack," Nawautin replied, and he wiped his face.

"I'm almost sure that I heard another voice besides yours," Puwaugun insisted. He set about unloading his canoe.

"Father! I killed a rabbit," Nawautin suddenly exclaimed, his voice strong with pride. "I cleaned it and cooked it too," he added.

Puwaugun placed his hand on his son's shoulder. He was proud.

"I'm glad. You're going to be a good hunter. Before you know it, you'll be going with me. And you made a fire ... and cooked it too?" he asked, scarcely believing what he had heard.

Nawautin said nothing.

The next morning, as he was leaving, Puwaugun told his son that instead of taking the canoe, he was going to walk straight back into the forest behind their lodge.

Anxiously, Nawautin watched his father disappear beyond the knoll. Then, as quickly as his legs could carry him, Nawautin was beside the oak. "He's gone. You can come out now," he said.

Waematik's face appeared on the surface of the tree. He seemed reluctant to come out. "Are you sure?"

"Yes! He's gone. He won't be back for a while. Anyway, you'll know when he is coming." Slowly Waematik came out.

To start their day, Waematik taught Nawautin the plum stone game. Each boy tried to guess how many stones the other had concealed under a wooden bowl. With each wrong guess, they yelled out and burst into laughter.

But they had scarcely begun when Waematik's countenance changed. "Someone's coming! Your father! I must go!" he exclaimed. He dropped the plum stones, rose quickly, turned and gasped.

There, by the great oak, stood Puwaugun.

Waematik had nowhere to run. His voice broke as he pleaded, "Don't hurt me. Don't hurt me. I don't mean any harm." His whole being trembled.

Nawautin, afraid to lose his friend and stirred by his friend's terror, ran to his father. "Father! Don't hurt him. He's my friend. Let him stay."

Very deliberately, Puwaugun assured his son, "I have no reason to hurt your friend. You need not fear so. He can stay if he wants." He could not take his eyes off the strange little boy. There was something familiar about him which at first eluded Puwaugun, but as he continued to study Waematik, he recognized the features, manners and voice of Waubizee-quae, his wife and the mother of Nawautin. She had come back in the form of a little boy to care for their son.

One morning two years later, after he had played many games and learned many hunting skills, Nawautin did as he had done every day — he ran to the oak to summon his friend to play. But there was no answer and no Waematik, that day nor ever again.

The Sound of Dancing

(as told by Earth Elder,
and retold by Alexander Wolfe)

"Grandfather Earth Elder, to whom I am deeply
indebted, was born at a time when, as he described it,
'no white man was seen, only heard about.' He also
said about himself, 'I was forty winters old when we
went to the valley (QuAppelle) to discuss the treaties.'
Then, of course, there is his most profound statement
to me, which was also his last. Grandfather, who on
that August day in 1937 was deaf, nearly blind, with the
last of his teeth gone, stooped and unable to walk — he
could only shuffle very slowly — but whose mind was
clear, said these words: 'Machan noosis [Go grandson],
do not look back, follow the path before you, it goes far
into the future.' Grandfather's age was estimated at
107 at the time of his passing, an age seldom reached
by any member of his band.

    Grandfather Earth Elder and the other grandfathers
of his day were the bearers of the oral tradition. Within
the oral tradition were the stories, songs and family
history as experienced by each succeeding generation.
Within a short time after we of our generation became
adults and had families of our own. Our parents passed

on. The time had come for us to assume responsibility for the continuation of the family stories and history. We had been told that the family stories and history must continue, to preserve the identity, the responsibilities, of future generations. We as adults and heads of our own families knew that a critical time in the history of our people had arrived. Our children had no knowledge of the language in which we adults had been raised. The descendants of the great, great grandfather Pinayzitt had become so numerous, they numbered several hundred and were scattered over a large area. Many of the young within this large group had no idea of their relationship to each other and their extended family background.

Because of all this, it was decided to break the age-old oral tradition, and use the written word. Due to the loss of language, this was the only way to ensure the continuation of the family stories and to preserve our history. This transition from oral to written word took a number of years. We were fortunate that a number of the older members of certain families still spoke the original language of the grandfathers. This helped in the translation of words and the original names of places — names that are not in use anymore. We were also fortunate in that two aunts were still living and these ladies helped verify the families and the stories. At this time, one has reached her hundreth birthday, and the other is ninety-eight. They are the granddaughters of the original grandfather, Pinayzitt. Our purpose at first was to record the stories and the times of our grandfathers for family information, not for publication. The writing was almost complete at the time when much emphasis was being placed on Indian control of education. This trend altered the purpose for which the stories were intended and the Earth Elder stories became a published book (*Earth Elder Stories*, Fifth House).

As the writer, it was my hope that other families would tell the stories and eventually those of us involved in Indian control of education would have something that was truly ours. Indian control of education, in my thinking, is what you put into it, not what you borrow from someone else. Within the oral tradition there is philosophy, history, moral ethics and the whole of life. The principles contained within the oral tradition are adaptable to any age and time, so long as there are people.

The first three stories in the book lay down the principles which provide the foundation that governs the behaviour of aboriginal people socially and spiritually. The story *Sound of Dancing* is one that tells why a certain belief and custom is observed. It tells how that belief came into being and places a custom that is followed today within its cultural and spiritual tradition. There are other stories of this nature, but this story was always used and told by our grandfathers.

I hope that in reading this story, people may have deeper insight into why Indian people to this day gather to share what they have, and why eating together is so important. It has been said by the grandfathers that sharing does not end here, but is carried into the world of spirituality. In our time, we must be responsible to those who left behind so much. Credit for this story goes to the grandfathers who told it and used it to show how we must be responsible."

▼▼▼

Many years ago when Indians roamed this land, hunting and gathering for their survival, it was not uncommon for small groups to fall victim to raiding parties of hostile Indians of other tribes. The following account is of one little boy who survived to tell the tale of what happened to his people.

The camp was small. It was winter when the attack came, so ferocious that there was no hope of survival. The grandfather, covered only with a buffalo robe, fled with his grandson in hand. Their flight was short-lived as the grandfather was soon struck down by blows. In a last attempt to save his grandson, he grabbed him and threw himself on top of the boy, covering both of them with his buffalo robe.

As time went by, everything became quiet.

The boy asked his grandfather, "How long will we be here?"

The grandfather answered, "I will try to keep you as long as I can."

With this the boy fell asleep lying under the robe with his grandfather. In time the boy awoke. He could hear his grandfather talking with people, as if they were visiting. He wondered who they were, but did not dare ask his grandfather, because he knew that when older people were speaking it was impolite to interrupt. One was supposed to listen and learn from what they spoke about. Again, he fell back to sleep. At times when the boy awoke all would be quiet, as if it were night, and again he would keep silent lest he waken Grandfather, who was asleep. It was at these quiet times that he could hear in the distance the sounds of a drum with people singing, the sounds of people as they danced, and people speaking in remembrance of those gone before them. All this puzzled the boy, and at times when he awoke and Grandfather was awake he longed to ask him, but always Grandfather was talking to someone else.

After some time had gone by, the boy awoke again and all was quiet. He wondered, was it really nighttime? Why was it so quiet? Without disturbing Grandfather the boy slowly lifted the buffalo robe, just a tiny bit and peeked out. It was daylight. As the boy lay beside Grandfather he wondered what was happening to him and the place where they were. Again he heard Grandfather awaken and begin talking to others as he always did. The boy waited for the right time to speak, to ask Grandfather why there were times of quiet, why he heard in the distance people singing and speaking of those who were no longer with them. Why all these things? Even now Grandfather was speaking to someone, as if he was visiting. Yet he never left. How long was he to lie here beside his grandfather. Grandfather had said, "I will try to keep you as long as I can."

When the right time came and Grandfather was silent for a moment the boy spoke, "Grandfather, why is it there are times when everything is quiet and in the distance I hear people. Then at other times you seem awake, you talk to others as if you were visiting. Why all these things, and how long are we to be here?"

Grandfather spoke, "My grandson, the time has come for you to go. I have kept my promise for I have kept you as long as I could. Now you must leave. But first I will speak of the things you ask. When my day ends, you day begins. With that you must leave. When it is quiet it is my night, and I must begin to prepare for my next day, just as you must be quiet in your night and rest for your next day. Those that you hear in the distance are your people; they are in their day. It is their time to sing and dance, to remember those of us who are no longer there, to remember what we had to say about life and how it should be lived. You must tell all that I tell you to your people — to those who will accept your word, and even to those who will doubt you. You must remember how to use those things that are yours and to share with others, even with us who are here. The times when I speak to others here are during my day. There are many who are here. We also have our song and dance, and in time to come you will be here. For this reason your tears shall not flow when you leave here at the end of my day to begin your day. When you leave here you will go due south. After you have made four camps you will reach your people. Go, my grandson, it is time to begin your day and tell all that I have told you."

With this the boy lifted the buffalo robe which covered him and his grandfather. It was daylight. Spring had come. The snow had melted on the hills. Only the bushes and the low spots had snow. Gently he covered Grandfather, whom he now knew had been gone for many days. Grandfather's spirit had kept him warm and alive. As he looked at the remains of those who had fallen in the attack, he felt a lump in his throat, but Grandfather had said no tears should flow. He knew if he cried Grandfather would hear. Slowly the boy began to walk. He faced to the south. When evening came he made camp. In the quiet of the evening the boy remembered all that Grandfather had said. To the north the northern lights danced. He remembered grandfather's words: we also have our song and dance. On the morning of the fourth camp, as the boy walked along, he smelled wood smoke and, going further over a ridge, he sighted a camp. He had found his people.

When the boy told what his grandfather had said and how he had survived, there were some who questioned his story and demanded to see the place where the attack had taken place during the past winter. In this the boy saw Grandfather's words coming true because he had said there would be those who did not accept his story of survival. In due time the boy led a group of men to the site. There they found the remains of those who had died in the attack. Grandfather still lay there covered with the buffalo robe, as the grandson had left him.

Tellers'
Tales

Voiceover

The job of a storyteller is not only to make us laugh, or cry, or dream; he or she must also remind us that all things, both stories and lives, must one day come to an end. The storyteller prepares us for the ending of things by telling us of new beginnings. The great clown Grimaldi wants to die, and must learn to out-clown his own sadness; Ken Roberts had a real-life experience of his own near death, and he carried the memory of it into his adult life. Storytellers teach us that wisdom often comes from suffering. Andrew, the Dene trapper, tells how his wolves grew from cubs and ran back to the wilderness one day. Now that this sad moment has turned into a story, he can remember without bitterness both his joy as well as his sorrow.

Stories end, say the storytellers, but not our love for them. People die, but not our memory of them. As one African proverb tells us: A person is not dead unless they have been forgotten.

▼▼▼▼▼▼

How to Tell a Story

Robert Minden

"When I tell stories from the stage, I make music or,
perhaps, when I play music from the stage I tell stories.
Sometimes the stories are a part of the music and
sometimes the music belongs to the story. The stories
usually come from my life, moments that marked me or
changed me in some mysterious way. Perhaps they are
memoirs, these stories. Sometimes they begin as a
memory and become imaginings. This means that there
a limited number of stories that I can tell. I have always
found it difficult to tell stories that didn't belong to me.
But sometimes I cross paths with a story that resonates
and I find that I am telling this story to myself and then
to others. This story becomes part of me, like a whisper
in my ear."

▼▼▼

Once, a rabbi was asked: "Rabbi, how do you tell a story?"

And the rabbi answered: "A story should be told in such
a way that the very telling offers help. My grandfather, my
zaida, had been a disciple of the Baal Shem, the 'Master of
the Good Name,' the founder of Hasidism. My grandfather
was lame. He hadn't walked in years. One day some of his

students asked him to tell a story about his famous teacher, and he began to tell how his teacher, the Baal Shem, would pray.

'As he began his prayer,' my grandfather said, 'the Baal Shem would begin to sway. And then he would hop — first on one foot, and then on the other, and finally turn himself into dance.' And as my grandfather told this story, he rose out of his chair and began to hop — first on one foot, then on the other. He began to hop and dance to show what the master had done. And from that moment on, he was never lame again. That's how to tell a story!"

Grimaldi

Carmen Orlandis-Habsburgo

"I was born in Spain, the eldest of eight siblings and the black sheep of the family. I do things upside down, to go up I go down, to go in I go out, always spinning about.

Crazy? Yes, I am. Are you not? I am the bottom and the top, the queen of the fools, I can do anything I want, even dust off the Emperor of the World, if there was one and I wished to do so. It is good for a man to remember that he still sits on his seat way up on the throne.

I am the mocker and the mocked, the victim and the tormentor, a shape changer, a trickster … I juggle emotions like other people juggle balls and I know how to use a hammer to make people whole.

Lady, are you real? I am, real or not! I am a professional clown, true magic or false illusion, it depends whether the Spirit is there or not; when the magic is not there and I must do my job, experience fills in to make the illusion work. But there is a price to be paid whenever I paint the clown on my face and the Spirit does not answer the call. And, while I sit in the hole, I think of those great performers who had what I have not: I think of Grimaldi."

Over a hundred years ago, Grimaldi was the best clown in the world. When Grimaldi entered the circus ring, the crowd roared with laughter and they laughed and they laughed till tears rolled down their cheeks and they forgot all their sorrows. Grimaldi never failed to amuse the crowds. At the end of his act, the women would cover him with flowers and the men with gold and silver coins. And so it was that the circus grew prosperous, the dancing bears were fat, and the lion had a shiny coat.

One day, at the end of the summer, the circus reached the town of Vienna — the Imperial city, a happy place where beauty lived in people's hearts, a city famous for her music, her wine, her pastry and her doctors. Now, among these famous doctors, one was especially well known because he did not only treat sickness of the body but he could also heal the sickness of the soul.

Shortly after the arrival of the circus, an odd gentleman entered the office of the great doctor. He was dressed in an elegant fashion, with a silk top hat and a walking stick. He was tall and thin and the skin of his face clung closely to the bone. What was odd about him is hard to tell, but there was something in his eyes that made you shiver, as if you were looking into two dark pools of deep despair. This man asked to see the doctor and he was told that the doctor was very busy and he would have to wait at least three months.

"I can't wait!" he said, and he reached into his pocket and pulled out a fist full of golden coins; "I can't wait! I must see the doctor now!" And so it was that the odd gentleman entered the consultation room.

"What ails you, sir?" the doctor asked.

"Nothing … nothing ails me," he answered. "You will not find illness in my flesh … and still, I'm stale at work, I shy the company of my friends, I don't care for food, women, or drink. I feel myself sinking deeper and deeper into the blackness of my own death …"

"Sir," the doctor said, "you suffer from an acute form of melancholy … but you can be healed if you follow my instructions."

"I will follow them," replied the odd man.

"Very well," the doctor said. "Tonight you must go to the circus and see the clown Grimaldi."

"Grimaldi … ?" the odd man said. "If that is my only hope … I'm as good as dead!"

"Not so, my friend," the doctor said. "I believe that laughter breaks the melancholic spell. I have seen other patients recover that way from their afflictions. Last night, I went to see the clown myself. When Grimaldi entered the ring, we roared with laughter, and we laughed and we laughed till tears rolled down our cheeks and we forgot all our sorrows. It will not fail, trust me! Go and see Grimaldi!"

"Doctor," the odd man said, his eyes two deep pools of black despair, "I am Grimaldi!"

"Ah … !" the doctor said. "Then yours is truly a desperate case. You heard the Siren singing, and like all doomed sailors, you are heading inexorably towards your own destruction. Ah, my friend! Take my advice, if in the end you must do it, do it tonight and spare yourself the long agony!"

"I knew there was no escape!" Grimaldi said. "Doctor, will you at least provide me with the means to die a peaceful death?"

"Far from it!" the doctor answered. "Tonight, under the circus tent, for all to see, you must die the most violent of deaths!"

"For all to see?" Grimaldi asked. And then there was a twinkle in his eye and a grin on his face. He reached into his pocket and he pulled out a fist full of golden coins.

That night, under the tent, the clown tried to kill himself. First he tried to cut his throat with a giant butcher knife; and he cut and he sliced, but somehow the knife refused to sink into his flesh. Then he tried to blow his brains out, and when he pulled the trigger the gun went up in smoke. Even before the smoke had cleared, he built a giant scaffold and hanged himself by the neck — and while he was kicking the air, the hanging rope broke and the clown hit the ground. More determined than ever to die, he climbed the high trapeze and, for all to see, jumped fearlessly into the void — to be saved by his suspenders. The crowd roared with laughter! And they say that night was the only time Grimaldi could not keep a straight face. Before the end of his hundred futile deaths, he joined the crowd in laughter; and he laughed and he laughed till tears rolled down his cheeks and he forgot all his sorrows.

▼▼▼▼▼▼

Almost Dying

Ken Roberts

"Most of the stories I write and tell have a strong
element of humour. I love to stretch reality. *Almost
Dying* is an exception.

I first wrote *Almost Dying* in 1975, one year after
having found the body of a friend who committed
suicide. The story has changed little since then.

Almost Dying tricks people. It establishes an
atmosphere of warmth into which horror is quickly and
chillingly inserted. The only problem I have ever found
with this particular story is that, once told, I must take a
break before telling anything else. Because of its
autobiographical nature, *Almost Dying* requires me to
pull out my emotions, poke a sword at them, and force
them to walk the plank. There is no easy return."

▼▼▼

When I was six years old I put a knife in my forehead. My
mother had warned me that knives are dangerous, so when
a boy from down the street came up the street with a knife in
his hands, I nabbed it from him and ran to show Mom.

I kept both eyes on that knife. I didn't want it to leap up
and hurt me.

I kept both eyes on that knife and I didn't see the tree root and I tripped on the tree root and, since I was holding onto that knife so tightly, the blade slid into my forehead.

It sounds worse than it was. There is hard bone in the human skull.

My mother screamed when she saw me, though, and she bundled me up, put me in the car, and drove to our church. It was a Saturday, and my father was working on the church roof.

I've wondered about that since then — I mean why my mother drove to the church instead of driving straight to the hospital. She must have known it was an innocent wound.

Mom braked in front of the church. My father walked over to the edge of the roof, curious, a hammer in his hand. I was lying down in the back seat holding a towel to my head, but I could see him.

Mom slid over to the passenger seat and yelled out the window — "Ken just stabbed himself in the head with a knife!"

And then — and this is the most memorable moment of my entire childhood — my father jumped off that two-storey-tall roof.

He jumped off that roof even though there was a ladder next to him. He jumped off that roof because his youngest son, whom he loved — as proven by the fact that he jumped off that roof even though there was a ladder next to him — had just stabbed himself in the head with a rather small (he didn't know that), rather dull knife.

So … the image I see when I think of childhood is of my father halfway down that two-storey-tall church, his arms extended like a soaring bird. I remember the look on his face too, and it was fear.

I suppose it could have been fear about what was going to happen when he finally hit the ground, but I don't think so and I didn't think so then. I thought, and still do think, that it was fear for the life of his youngest son.

I don't remember what did happen when Dad hit the ground. I know he didn't hurt himself, because he drove the car to the hospital while my mother cradled my head in the back seat.

In the hospital emergency room, the doctor told my parents I had almost died. He said that if that blade had hit an inch or two to either side it could have pierced my brain and killed me. I was conscious, super-conscious really, and I saw my father and mother hug each other and cry and felt them both hug me ... and almost dying was wonderful. Everyone should almost die that way.

Everyone can't almost die that way, though. It isn't something you can plan.

I had a friend who tried. Colin took his drugs, turned up the stereo, and left his apartment door half open. Colin tried to almost die but not be hurt. Colin tried to almost die so the doctors could pump out his stomach and call his parents. Colin tried to almost die so he could watch his parents hug each other and cry as the doctor told them "Colin almost died."

Colin tried to almost die so he could feel loved and needed and ... damn you, Colin ... you discovered why everyone can't almost die to feel such emotions. You died, Colin. You died and felt nothing. I saw your parents hug each other and cry but you didn't.

You planned what I didn't plan, and you died while I, by accident, was given a gift of love and a vertical scar which, with age, has become a deep yet welcomed wrinkle.

▼▼▼▼▼▼

Andrew's Wolf Pups
René Fumoleau

"Andrew was about one year younger than me — a
Chipewyan Indian, born on the southern shore of Great
Slave Lake ('Tutcho'). He lived and trapped and worked
in the small village of Rocher River. In the 1950s and
1960s the Government forced or bribed a lot of Dene
into abandoning their small villages and communities
and moving into larger centres, towns, or cities —
allegedly so they could get better 'services,' but in fact
to move the Dene out of their traditional lands so that
1) these lands would be available for exploitation, and
2) the Dene would abandon their traditions, and
therefore 3) they could be more easily controlled.
Andrew himself moved, like many of his friends, from
a prosperous, self-contained, self-governing
community, with plenty of fish, meat, and fur, into
Yellowknife, where there is really no place for Dene
and Aboriginal people, unless they want to become
'white' — and forget who they are.

He lived on the fringe, worked now and then,
stayed with his mother (who was blind) until she died
in the mid-1970s. He had a very little shack (one stove,
one bed, one water barrel). In the late 1970s he was

going away for a few days; he let somebody stay in his house when he was away; the house was burned down. He couldn't rebuild it because of city regulations which promoted the disappearance of small units and their replacement by sumptuous big houses for the rich.

So Andrew lived here and there, at the Salvation Army or similar kinds of organizations and people. He showed up at my place two or three times a week for breakfast. That's when he told me many stories. He was crippled in an accident a few years ago, and walked with one crutch. In the summer of 1989, when he was out one night with a few friends, he was stabbed in the leg, lost too much blood, was in hospital for two or three days and died — the victim of what politicians and business people call 'the negative impact of development.'

As for me, I was ordained a priest in France in 1952, came to Denendeh in 1953, to Fort Good Hope in 1953-60, to Fort Franklin 1960-68, to Fort Good Hope again in 1968-69, and have been in Yellowknife since 1970, travelling here and there, doing a bit of this and that. Some people call me the 'freelance priest!' I have had a wonderful life in Denendeh."

▼▼▼

This morning, over breakfast, Andrew told me:

Years ago, me and my friend,
we were hunting near the Barren Land,
and we found five wolf pups in a den.

I had always dreamed of using wolves to pull my
    toboggan.
You know, wolves are so fast!
Well, this was my chance, my dream come true.

It was easy to pick up the pups,
but I didn't know much how to raise them,
or what to feed them.
For a while, they seemed to lose weight,
but they started to grow up again,
and then, they surely grew up fast.
Even as pups, they had such long legs!

Well, I was taking good care of them.
I wanted them to be so strong.
What a team they would make! ... and I would be
    so proud!
I always had good dogs ... but that team would be
    the best.
My God, I was so anxious to see them grow up.

I built a corral for them,
and five small houses,
each with a thick floor of spruce boughs.
I fed them the best fish I caught,
and even caribou meat.
My friends came to see my pups,
and I think they were kind of jealous of me.

Well, pretty soon, my pups were real grown-ups.
They stood taller than any dog I had ever had,
and their bodies were so, so long.
Boy! I was going to make good speed with them!

I bought a new set of harness,
and I mean first quality leather.

The first time I put them in the harness,
they jumped around, like all pups do,
and they seemed to wonder what was happening.
But I talked to them nicely,
and I even caressed them,
what I had never done to any dog before.

Slowly they got used to pulling the toboggan.
And you should have seen that speed!
To tell the truth, I treated them very well also.
I wanted them to be in top shape,
with strong muscles, and just enough fat;
and they were just like that.

Every night when we stopped in the bush,
I cut spruce boughs for them to sleep on,
and I always fed them before eating myself.
A few times, when I was short of food,
I even fed them what was supposed to be my supper.
But I was not sorry for treating them so well,
because they served me rightly,
and they pulled my toboggan on many trips.

They were nearly two years old
when I travelled to the Barren Land with them,
to set a few traps, and to shoot a few caribou.
On the second day I put them in the harness,
just as I had done dozens of times.
But one started to pull right and left,
and pretty soon the five of them were jumping all over.

Before I could even think what to do,
one had chewed off his harness,
and all of them, in a flash, did the same,
dashed away, and disappeared beyond a hill.

I couldn't even get angry at them,
I knew this land so well,
I was sure I could make it home.
But I felt so sorry for my five dogs, no, my wolves.

Nobody would ever bring them food,
and I meant good food, and at the right time.
Now, they would have to roam all over in search of
    food,
and they would probably go hungry at times.

Nobody would caress them again,
and tell them soft and encouraging words.
Now, they were on their own in a freezing and desolate
    world.

Nobody would bring them spruce boughs to sleep on.
Now, they would have to face the blizzards, and the
    cruel winters.

Nobody would ever care for them,
Now, they would have to rely only on themselves.

What a tragedy for such fine animals
which had been treated so well,
I could even say, which had been loved so much.

As I walked and walked
I felt so sorry for them ...
until one day I stopped on the trail.
I shook my head, and said to myself:
"But anyway, now they are free."

Biographical Notes

▸ *Steve Altstedter* is a Toronto teacher who uses storytelling in his classroom program. He taught and coached Judo and is presently on the executive of the Dramatic Arts Network for Toronto Schools.

▸ *Pat Andrews* is a unique and well-known storyteller, writer and artist who grew up on a wilderness lake in Northern Ontario. Throughout all of her work runs her love of stories and of nature. She lives in rural Ontario.

▸ *Bob Barton* is a freelance storyteller and writer. His books include *Tell Me Another* (Pembroke: 1986), *Stories To Tell* (Pembroke: 1992), *The Reindeer Herder and the Moon* (Longman: 1993) and *The Storm Wife* (Quarry: 1993). He is one of the original founders of the Storytellers School of Toronto.

▸ *Jocelyn Bérubé* was born in 1946 in Saint-Nil in the Gaspé region. In 1969 he became one of the founding members of "Le Grand Cirque Ordinaire," a collective creation troupe. Since 1971 he has put on many shows as a storyteller and musician in Quebec and throughout Europe and the United States.

▸ *Louis Bird* is a distinguished elder of the Omushkigo (Cree). He was born on the western shores of James Bay, at Winisk. After his village was flooded, the entire community moved to Peawanuck, where Louis lives to this day. For the last three decades, Louis has worked diligently to preserve the oral history of his people and their land, and to keep alive their traditional stories. He is a popular performer at cultural and storytelling festivals around the country.

▶ *Teresa Doyle* is known primarily as a singer, and has appeared regularly at folk festivals and concert halls in Canada, Europe and Japan during her fifteen-year career. Her latest recording, *Stowaway*, is a collection of original and traditional songs that pays tribute to the early settlers of Prince Edward Island. Teresa lives in Belfast, Prince Edward Island.

▶ *Bernadette Dyer* was born in Kingston, Jamaica and was educated in both Jamaica and Canada. She lives in Toronto and works for Toronto Public Libraries in children's services. She is a storyteller and artist, and has had many poems and short stories published in little magazines throughout Canada.

▶ *J. Antonin Friolet* is a well-known raconteur and chronicler of life in New Brunswick.

▶ *René Fumoleau* lives in Yellowknife, Northwest Territories.

▶ *Nan Gregory* has been a professional storyteller since 1984. She lives in Vancouver.

▶ *Lynda Howes* began her life-involvement with storytelling upon hearing the wonder tales of Old Mother Russia. She contributed to *Tales for an Unknown City* (McGill-Queens University Press: 1990), a collection of stories edited by Dan Yashinsky. In collaboration with Celia Barker Lottridge, Lynda Howes created and performed "A Feast in Arthur's Hall," stories from the Mabinogion. She grew up in rural Saskatchewan, and currently lives in Toronto.

▶ *Esther Jacko* has been handed down Ojibway stories and legends from her grandparents since childhood, through the oral traditions of storytelling. Realizing the cultural and historical significance of these stories prompted her to preserve and continue this oral tradition with her own children and their friends. Soon the circle widened to include community, schools and theatre groups. The stories that she shares teach about the Ojibway way of life of long ago — its cultural beliefs, value system and history upon the land. These stories are also an explanation of how the Ojibway perceived their relationship with nature. Ms. Jacko has adapted several of her stories into plays and has had some of her work published. She lives in Birch Island, Ontario.

▸ **Basil Johnston,** O. Ont., is the author of many books on Ojibway heritage, as well as an autobiography entitled *Indian School Days* (Key Porter: 1988). He is a lecturer at the Royal Ontario Museum in the Ethnology Department.

▸ **Lenore Keeshig-Tobias** is an award-winning author and storyteller. She was born on the Neyaashiinigmiing (Cape Croker) reserve in Ontario, where she now lives. She has three grown daughters, a grandson, and a young daughter and son. As a culture worker, she has worked on anti-racism in the arts, particularly through the issue of cultural appropriation. She shares the 1993 "Living the Dream Award" with her daughter Polly, for their book *Bird Talk* (Sister Vision: 1991).

▸ **Justin Lewis** grew up hearing folk tales from his parents and reading their many books. Besides telling, translating and writing stories, he studies and teaches Jewish lore and legend. He lives in Toronto with his wife, singer-storyteller Jane Enkin.

▸ **Frieda Ling** is the Children's and Young People's Services Coordinator of the Toronto Public Library, and a storyteller specializing in Chinese literary tales for adults. She is also co-director of the course "Children's Literature: A Multicultural Perspective" at York University.

▸ **Celia Barker Lottridge** is a Toronto storyteller, Director of the Parent-Child Mother Goose Program and the author of many books, including *The Name of the Tree* (Groundwood: 1989), *Ticket to Curlew* (Groundwood: 1992) and *Ten Small Tales* (Groundwood: 1993).

▶ *Steve Luxton* was born in Coventry, England and now makes his home in Montreal, Quebec. He is a founder of an oral and narrative performance group called The Montreal Storytellers, and is an original editor of *The Moosehead Review*. As well, he has edited collections of short stories and poetry, and has published three books, *Late Romantics* (with Robert Allen and Mark Teicher, Moosehead: 1980), *The Hills That Pass By* (DC Books: 1987) and *Iridium* (DC Books: 1993).

▶ *Joe Neil MacNeil* has lived most of his life in Big Pond, Cape Breton. He has travelled to festivals throughout Canada and Scotland, telling traditional Gaelic stories. He is the author of *Tales Until Dawn* (McGill-Queens University Press: 1987).

▶ *Deanne Mallard* is a student at Trent University. She enrolled at Trent after a three-year hiatus between high school and university. In that time, she travelled extensively and worked to support her ventures. She continues to write and tell stories, and is presently working on a collection of children's tales.

▶ *Robert Minden's* background in several disciplines informs his work as a storyteller, composer and teacher. He studied piano and composition at the Royal Conservatory of Music in Toronto and then went on to pursue a career in sociology. After teaching at several universities, he began to focus his interests around photography, music and theatre. Investigations into acoustic sound and invented instruments, together with a love of storytelling, led to the formation of the Robert Minden Ensemble in 1986. The Ensemble, a quartet of found object and conventional instruments, tours its unusual productions of music theatre internationally. He lives in Vancouver.

- **Carmen Orlandis-Habsburgo** is descended from Spanish nobility. She works as a clown and lives in Toronto and Mexico.

- **Gilbert Oskaboose** is an Ojibway from the Serpent River First Nation in Northern Ontario. He is presently Communications Director for the North Shore Tribal Council. He has had many incarnations over the years, including Indian residential school survivor, hunting/fishing guide, hard rock miner, catskinner, deckhand, high-steel rigger, firefighter, editor, poet, hippie, trading post manager, parent and lover.

- **Marylyn Peringer** has been telling stories to young people and adults for more than fifteen years, and has visited hundreds of schools and libraries across Canada. Her storytelling interests include Greek and Roman mythology, folklore of the stars and constellations and especially the legends of French Canada, which she tells bilingually. She lives in Toronto.

- **Camille Perron** lives in Astorville, Ontario. He has shared stories from his Franco-Ontarian tradition at festivals throughout Canada.

- In 1984, **Melanie Ray** transformed herself from a talented but mostly unemployed actress into a talented and mostly employed storyteller. She was one-half of the Wives' Tales Story Tellers for over five years, then began working on her own. She feels very lucky to be making a living doing what she loves. She lives in Vancouver.

- **Ken Roberts** has written a number of novels for young people, including the bestselling *Hiccup Champion of the World* (Douglas and McIntyre: 1988). He has taught puppetry, drama, librarianship and children's literature at several Canadian universities. He lives in Whitby, Ontario.

- **Itah Sadu** is a fresh, dynamic storyteller and author with many voices. Her love of stories comes from her Barbadian mother and many hours of listening to gossip, memories, anecdotes and folk tales. She is the author of *Christopher, Please Clean Up Your Room* (Scholastic: 1993), and other children's books. She lives in Toronto.

▸ *John Shaw* is a folklorist. He is the translator and editor of Joe Neil MacNeil's book *Tales Until Dawn* (McGill-Queens University Press: 1987). He lives in Cape Breton and Scotland.

▸ *Kay Stone* is a folklorist who studies stories and also a storyteller who tells them. She teaches both folklore and storytelling techniques at the University of Winnipeg in Manitoba and has written several articles about stories and storytelling. If she had her own way, she would tell tales *all* the time, happily ever after.

▸ *Shawna Watson* is a storyteller who tells stories in French and English. She lives in Toronto.

▸ *Alexander Wolfe* is a Saulteaux storyteller and author of *Earth Elder Stories* (Fifth House: 1988), a collection of stories belonging to his family, who are the descendants of Pinayzitt (Partridge Foot). He spends much of his time in Saskatchewan.

▸ *Dan Yashinsky* founded the Toronto Festival of Storytelling. He is the editor of *Tales for an Unknown City* (McGill-Queens University Press: 1990) and the author of *The Storyteller at Fault* (Ragweed: 1992). He lives in Toronto.

▸ *Ricky Zurif* teaches English at Champlain College in St. Lambert, Quebec. She tells stories in her free time and enjoys it, but she is unwilling to give up her day job.

▼▼▼▼▼▼

The Best of Ragweed Press

▸ *Bigfoot Sabotage*, **Deirdre Kessler** When a logging operation threatens to destroy the forest and expose the cave that shelters the fabled Bigfoot, Maya and her brother Jake must make tough decisions about taking the law into their own hands.   ISBN 0-921556-19-5 $6.95

▸ *Brupp Rides Again*, **Deirdre Kessler** Everyone's favourite cat is back, this time on a western adventure. Brupp hops a boxcar to the great western prairie, where he befriends a gang of runaway children.   ISBN 0-921556-33-0 $6.95

▸ *Bud the Spud*, **Stompin' Tom Connors, illustrated by Brenda Jones** Here is Stompin' Tom Connors' famous and irresistible song about potatoes in lively storybook form. Travel with Bud as he steers his rig down the highway with a load of "the best doggone potatoes that's ever been growed."
                                                                 ISBN 0-921556-43-8 $5.95

▸ *Dancing at the Club Holocaust: Stories New & Selected*, **J.J. Steinfeld** This is Steinfeld's most powerful collection, gathering the best of his writing—stories about North American Jewish experience.   ISBN 0-921556-30-6 $14.95

▸ *From Red Clay & Salt Water: Prince Edward Island & Its People*, **John Sylvester** Eighty colour photographs and eighteen fascinating interviews combine to form a revealing portrait of the Island, and give eloquent testimony to the links between environment and culture, land and heart, in the "Garden of the Gulf." ISBN 0-921556-40-3 $24.95

▶ *An Island Alphabet*, **Erica Rutherford** In this beautiful alphabet book, Erica Rutherford's bright, evocative paintings illustrate both familiar and unusual features of Prince Edward Island life. ISBN 0-951556-44-6 $14.95

▶ *Lnu and Indians We're Called*, **Rita Joe** Micmac poet Rita Joe's third collection of poetry follows and expands upon her desire to communicate gently with her own people and to reach out to the wider community. ISBN 0-921556-22-5 $9.95

▶ *Mogul and Me*, **Peter Cumming, illustrated by P. John Burden** Based on a true story, this dramatic tale of the friendship between a New Brunswick farmboy and a circus elephant is also a story of love and trust, of good and evil. ISBN 0-920304-82-6 $8.95

▶ *The Storyteller at Fault*, **Dan Yashinsky** A masterful tale of adventure, wit and suspense, by an accomplished raconteur. Folk literature and oral traditions from around the world are woven into a colourful tapestry that is a whole new tale in itself. ISBN 0-921556-29-2 $9.95

RAGWEED PRESS books can be found in quality bookstores, or individual orders may be sent prepaid to: **RAGWEED PRESS**, P.O. Box 2023, Charlottetown, Prince Edward Island, Canada, C1A 7N7. Please add postage and handling ($2.45 for the first book and 75 cents for each additional book) to your order. Canadian residents add 7% GST to the total amount. GST registration number R104383120.